DEATH ON THE PEDERNALES

Book Three in the Series

The Trail of Blood and Wine

PAUL AND MERRILL BONARRIGO

Death on the Pedernales
Book Three in the Series
Trails of Blood and Wine

Publisher: Merbon
4401 Old Reliance Road
Bryan, Texas 77808
979-820-1238

Mer-Bon.com/story/
@mer-bon
@TheVineyardDistrict

Copyeditor and Cover Design: Abby Parker
Soft Cover ISBN 978-1-7361770-5-1
eBook ISBN: 978-1-7361770-6-8

To Paul and Karen Bonarrigo,

To our grandchildren

Paul Anthony and Sophia Marie Bonarrigo,

the next generation of Texas wine pioneers,

and

To the Lord who has so blessed us.

May the Lord forever bless you and guide your
paths.

*"I am the vine; you are the branches. If you
abide in me and I in you, you will bear much
fruit; apart from me you can do nothing."*

John 15:5

Death on the Pedernales

Chapter 1

There is nothing like a glorious Texas Hill Country morning - the rolling hills, the clear limestone- bottom streams, the wildflowers with their color palate of red, white, and blue, the smell of honeysuckle, and the morning dew on the lavender. How could life be more perfect than living in the Texas Hill Country? Fredericksburg, Texas, was to become our new home.

My name is John Boone. I moved my family down to Texas from New York. My wife, Joann, and I grew up there. I attended Columbia University, where I studied computer science. It was a huge blessing that I received a scholarship. Otherwise, my family could not have afforded my Ivy League education.

While a junior at Columbia, I played in a rock-and-roll band called "The Plague". We played fraternity and sorority parties all over New York, New Jersey, and Connecticut. We also played at the Bitter End in "The Village". Joann was in the audience. I noticed her red hair but did not have the courage to say hello. A week later, the band was playing at the Night Owl down the street. Joann was sitting in the first row of tables. She looked beautiful and exuded an exciting personality. This time, I mustered the courage to introduce myself. As I approached her, she stood up. She was about five foot four with an hourglass figure. My heart started beating faster as she leaned toward me to shake my hand. Her lovely blue eyes seemed to look right through me. Her voice was like that of an angel.

It was the best thing that I had ever done. The greatest benefit of that rock and roll period of my life was meeting my beautiful wife, Joann.

She is the most positive person I have ever known. If it were not for her positivity, I would never have made it through Columbia. She was attending New York University and studying to become a teacher.

Since that time, we have done everything together. We studied together, laughed together, and shared love together. Life in school and in New York can be very difficult but when you are with the one you love, it is a time of wonder and excitement. After graduating we stayed in New York.

I got a job working at IBM in Armonk, New York, a small community of 4,000 people thirty-seven miles north of Manhattan. Joann worked as a seventh-grade teacher in Byrom Hills Central School District. Two to three times per month we would drive into the city for dinner and show. Life was grand.

Our favorite getaway was going to the glacially carved Finger Lakes and visiting wineries nestled in the heart of New York. The region is 9,000 square miles. It captivated our senses and refreshed our souls with its enchanting landscapes of lush green hills, crystal clear lakes, and quaint little towns. The name was inspired because the lakes resemble five fingers on a hand. Each of the lakes Cayuga, Seneca, Keuka, Canandaigua, and Skaneateles sparkle like jewels against the evergreen canvas.

The wine lifestyle so inspired us that we joined a wine club called "The Knights of the Vine". Through them we learned so much about wines of the world but especially became fond of the wines of New York.

For example, did you know that Seneca Lake is the deepest and second longest of the Finger Lakes? They say that due to its depth, it does not freeze easily and provides a more moderate temperature for the grapes above its banks. Most people do not know that the majestic Taughannock Falls are two hundred fifteen feet high, which makes them higher than Niagara Falls.

The lakes are oriented north to south. We enjoyed beautiful sunrises and sunsets from both sides of the lakes and loved visiting the farmers' markets in the rolling hills of the countryside, where they sold fresh produce from the apple and cherry orchards and the vineyards.

The winemakers told us that the soil is rich; the hills drain down to the lakes, and the lakes provide what is known as the "lake effect" on the vines. Warm, moist air rises from the warmer lake water, resulting in a lower risk of freezing temperatures for the vines.

The history of winemaking in the Finger Lakes dates back to the nineteenth century. Italian and German immigrants settled the area and continued the winemaking traditions of their fatherlands. The Finger Lakes were known for growing world-renowned Riesling, which was a traditional grape of Germany. Winemakers like Dr. Konstantin Frank promoted European grapes, especially Riesling, to be grown in the Finger Lakes.

Herman Weimer started one of the first grape nurseries in the eastern USA. Ben Riccardi has made Pinot Noir popular, and Nathan Kendall has developed some wonderful Chardonnay. New York was the largest producer of American wine before California took over after prohibition.

At a Knights of the Vine event, my wife Joann fell in love with the Riesling and Chardonnay. I was a fan of Finger Lakes Pinot Noir. Our host shared, "Our greatest concern is related to cold weather. The growers have trouble with winter killing the plants. In the spring they are afraid of spring freeze when the new buds are destroyed by subfreezing spring weather. Finally, Finger Lake grape growers are concerned that the summer could be too cold, and the fruit would not ripen."

Joann and I sat on the patio of Hermann Winery overlooking Seneca Lake, marveling at how beautiful and tranquil the vistas were. Joann laughed and looked at me, saying, "We are not alone; the grapes do not like cold either." That was the moment we realized we loved New York state and its beauty, but Joann and I were ready to leave the cold and go south to enjoy warm weather.

The cold winters in Armonk begin around Thanksgiving and continue until late March. We have almost three months of below freezing weather. Often the roads are covered in snow. Traffic jams are common and very dangerous. Many businesses close and do not reopen until late March or April. I do admit the changing colors of the fall leaves are beautiful.

The summers are hot and humid. Our home in Armonk is not air-conditioned so when it gets hot and humid it is very uncomfortable.

Chapter 2

IBM sent me to a meeting in San Antonio, Texas. What an interesting and historic city! I walked on the River Walk and down to the Alamo Plaza. The Alamo is a UNESCO World Heritage Site. I visited San Fernando Cathedral built in 1731.

My most wonderful experience was visiting the Alamo. When I was a child, Davy Crockett and James Bowie were my heroes. I was honored to be in a place where two hundred great Texans defended Texas against members of the Mexican Army.

In my imagination, the Alamo was still a mission in the middle of a barren land, like the 1960 movie, *Alamo* starring John Wayne. It was so strange to see it sitting in the middle of downtown San Antonio. Once inside I could block out the surrounding commercial development and fantasize what those brave defenders must have experienced.

I toured the Culinary Institute in San Antonio and fell in love with Texas hospitality. Exploring the area, I drove to Fredericksburg, Texas, a quaint German community in the Hill Country only one hour away. Along the way deer bounded across the road.

I love to hunt. I was amazed to see so many deer roaming around Hill Country. It was impressive to learn that one of the best places in Texas to hunt deer is Hill Country.

There, I met Chef Ross at the Cabernet Grill and enjoyed great food and an impressive wine list. Joann and I love festivals. Fredericksburg and Gillespie County host many events and festivals throughout the year.

I called Joann and told her, "This just seems to be the perfect place for us. It has everything we love, plus warm weather!"

Joann and I love the seasons in the north, but we became tired of the very cold winters and my crazy neighbors.

When I presented the idea of moving to Texas she spoke thoughtfully, "What about the cool summers here and the stunning autumn when the leaves turn brilliant red-orange and golden yellow. People from all over the world travel to witness the kaleidoscope of color that we enjoy every morning from our home in New England.

"Plus, you love your winter sports," she continued. "Skiing, ice skating, ice fishing and sledding are just down the road. Will you miss it?"

These were all good questions. I did hate leaving the beautiful area we had grown to love, but I had spent the last twenty years working for a large computer company and was ready to enjoy the good life in the Texas Hill Country.

"Joann, you and I love to garden. In Texas you can garden all year long. We can grow figs without having to cover them in the winter. We may be able to grow olives. You love herbs and wildflowers. We can seed blue bonnets so that in the spring we will have a carpet of blue all around the house.

"The music scene is amazing. Austin is only one hour away, and Austin is known for its live music. The Texas wine industry is centered in Fredericksburg and there are festivals almost every weekend.

"Did you know there are more than one hundred seventy-five wineries within twenty miles of Fredericksburg? The Finger lakes boast one hundred forty wineries. Fredericksburg has the second most wine tourists in the United States. Napa is the only place with more.

"Texans are very friendly people. We will make new friends. It will be a good life. I know we will be happy there. The warmer climate will allow us to be much more active throughout the year."

I was ready to retire and move to Texas.

Chapter 3

Driving from New York to Texas in a rented Ryder Truck, we took our time and discovered treasures along the way. Our first stop was to drive to the Bronx and see 'Little Italy'.

On 182nd Street, I drove passed Mt. Carmel Catholic Church and tried to turn left on Arthur Ave. The steering wheel was stuck. The steering would only make a full turn going right. The truck could not make a 90-degree left turn. So, every turn had to be a series of right turns just to go left. Several right turns later, we finally got to Arthur Ave.

The best New York pizza is the Half Moon Pizzeria. What truly distinguishes a great pizza is when you fold the enormous slice in half, and then you have to flip back the end point due to the weight of the cheese, the oil dripping down your arm as you bring the slice to your mouth and devour it. It was a sensual experience eating a Half Moon Pizza. Then we picked up cannolis at Artuso Pastry, the best pastry shop in the Bronx.

Leaving Arthur Ave. there was a left turn only. After pausing just long enough to realize the only other option was backing up in traffic, I grabbed the steering wheel and turned it left with all my might.

There was a loud pop. At first I thought I had broken the steering column. We took it to a gas station on Arthur Ave. The owner, Tiny Capello looked at the steering system and laughed out loud, saying, "A good yank always fixes everything."

Tiny was true to his name. He was a short slender man with his hair combed from left to right and his hands stained black from oil and grease. His smile filled his face. What a nice man! He did not even charge us.

Once he gave the truck an "ok", we took off and continued to Philadelphia, where we had the best Philly Cheese Steak. A Philly Cheese steak is made from thinly sliced beefsteak grilled with diced onions and thin pepper slices smothered with melted cheese on a long hoagie roll. The secrets are in the beef seasoning, the cheese blend, and the crusty bread with soft interior, and how it all melts in my mouth.

We were on a culinary journey. In Baltimore, we stopped to enjoy some good Maryland crab. Joann was eager to try half-smokes.

I asked, "What is that? I have never heard of it before."

She smiled and answered, "George Washington's signature dish was half-smokes, which is a combination of ground pork, beef, and spices smoked in a sausage casing. It is spicier than hot dogs. Didn't you learn that in history?"

"No, my history classes left out all to the fascinating culinary information!"

Our next stop was Rehoboth Beach, Delaware, for taffy. Every Christmas, we ordered taffy from the Holson Taffy Shop. We knew Rose and Frank were the owners, but we had never met them. This was a surprise visit to get taffy and hopefully meet them.

As we entered the store, we were enchanted by the sweet honeysuckle aromas that greeted us. There was a rainbow of color around the shop. Our mouths began to water.

"Can I help you?" said a jolly voice from behind the counter. It was Rose! We recognized her brown hair and rosy complexion from her photo on the store's website.

"Hello, we are John and Joanne Boone from New York. We are on our way to a new life and new adventures in Texas and wanted to stop by and introduce ourselves."

"What a pleasure to meet you! I recognize your names from your annual taffy shipments," said Rose.

"We love your taffy. Do you make it yourself?"

"Yes, my husband Frank and I make it." Frank was a tall slender friendly man with broad shoulders.

"You are famous. Everyone on the East Coast knows you as 'The Taffy Lady'."

As we were leaving with our choice of taffy, we thanked them and told them that we would continue to order from our new home in Texas. Rose said, "I have a brother in Texas. He is in the wine business. Be sure to look him up in Houston."

Atlanta was our next stop. Friends from my IBM days, Jeff and Diane Griffiths, had invited us to stay with them in their log cabin thirty miles north of Atlanta. It was our first time visiting.

"You live in the woods!" I yelled as we got out of our truck, which was parked on steep hill. There was even a fox sitting at the edge of the driveway. We could hear the woodpeckers hammering the trees next to the house.

They laughed, "Did you hear any banjoes on the way up the mountain? Our neighbor is a banjo player."

Diane was an Olympic figure skater. She even won a bronze medal.

They treated us to Georgia BBQ and peach cobbler. We asked Diane what sets Georgia BBQ apart from other BBQ. She told us, "Georgia and Carolina BBQ are usually pork, and the BBQ Sauce has ketchup, brown sugar, and mustard."

She continued, "Most Texas BBQ is beef that is slow-smoked over mesquite and hickory. You will have fun searching for the best Texas BBQ!"

Finally, our culinary adventure took us to New Orleans. There we met Chef Wight, the tallest chef I have ever met. His specialty, turtle soup, was the most amazing soup I had ever tasted. He invited us into the kitchen and even showed us how he prepared the soup begore giving us the recipe!

Turtle Soup

Ingredients
      12 tablespoons butter
      2 onions, diced
      6 stalks celery, diced
      20 cloves garlic, minced
      3 bell peppers, diced
      2 pounds turtle meat, diced
      1 tablespoon fresh thyme
      1 tablespoon fresh oregano
      5 bay leaves
      2 quarts veal stock
      1 cup all-purpose flour
      1 750 ml. bottle of Messina Hof Solera Sherry
      1 tablespoon tabasco sauce
      1/3 cup Worcestershire sauce
      2/3 cup Messina Hof Sauvignon Blanc

Directions:

1. In a large soup pot over medium heat, melt 4 ounces butter. Add onions, celery, garlic, and peppers. Stir until onions are translucent and garlic is aromatic.
2. Add turtle meat and cook until browned, constantly stirring. Add thyme, oregano and bay leaves. Sauté 15-20 minutes.
3. Add veal stock and simmer for 30 minutes.
4. Make roux. In a small saucepan, melt remaining butter over medium heat. Add flour very slowly, a little at a time, stirring constantly. Be careful not to burn as it thickens.
5. Keep stirring until all flour is incorporated and it begins to thicken with a nutty aroma. Set aside to cool before adding to soup.
6. Once the roux is cool, stir a small amount of soup stock into the roux to warm and begin to liquify. This will help prevent lumps. Slowly pour the roux into the soup stirring with a whisk. Simmer about 20 minutes, stirring to prevent burning on the bottom of the pan.
7. Add Solera Sherry and bring to boil. Add tabasco, Worcestershire sauce, and Sauvignon Blanc. Simmer another 10 minutes.

After an amazing evening of culinary delight, we drove to Houston, where we visited Messina Hof Harvest Green. Rose had recommended it. I was told they had the best pizza in Texas. As soon as we arrived, I saw the Napolitano pizza oven in the open concept kitchen. The whole kitchen staff had to be trained to use this fantastic Italian wood fired oven.

We ordered a Margarita pizza – my favorite. When it came to the table, my mouth watered. The cheese was perfectly melted, and the freshly harvested basil leaves were large and full of flavor. The crust was perfect. They said the sauce was from the owner's grandmother's recipe. They called it Mama Rosa's Marinara.

"Wow, they were right!" I exclaimed.

Joann looked at me and smiled, "You look surprised."

"New York pizza has nothing on this pizza. There is something about open fire pizza that cannot be matched in electric ovens. I just did not expect it. Mama Rosa must have been one of the best Italian chefs in Texas." I responded, "That sauce is the best!"

Chapter 4

The next morning was Thanksgiving. As we drove to the Hill Country, we saw wild turkey, dove, and quail. Joann laughed, "Our Thanksgiving turkey is coming to us!"

I told her I had a surprise for her. In Fredericksburg I took her to the Cabernet Grill and introduced her to my friend Chef Ross. He had reserved a table for us.

Joann was elated, "What a wonderful Thanksgiving surprise!"

Chef Ross introduced us to his wife Mariana. Joann could not resist asking, "How did you get into this business?"

Mariana shared, "We were both chefs. Ross began his career at the Westin Hotel in Dallas where we met and then journeyed to San Antonio as the executive sous chef of Cascabel Restaurant. Our love of Southwest Cuisine grew and when the Cabernet Grill became available for purchase, we jumped on it."

Ross chimed in, "We have cooked together for more than thirty years, and now our son, Hunter, has joined the team. He attended the Auguste Escoffier School of Culinary Arts and leads the day-to-day operations as our sous chef."

I complimented them on their food and their commitment to Texas wines. Ross brought over their wine director for introductions.

"You have put the Cabernet Grill on the map for some of Texas' finest cuisine," I remarked in between mouthfuls of delicious food.

It was deer season. There were deer everywhere. I love to hunt and this was a hunter's paradise. We checked into the Manor Haus at Messina Hof Hill Country.

"What a perfect place for relaxation after such a long trip," sighed Joann. I agreed.

The German style Haus was large and roomy with a living room, wet bar, large restroom, and king size bedroom. The bed was extra comfortable.

In our refrigerator we were surprised with a bottle of Messina Hof Sparkling wine and snacks. Joann grabbed two wine glasses, the wine, and my hand and led me out the back door to a patio overlooking a pond in the woods.

We sat there sipping our sparkling wine and enjoying the quiet calm of the patio. Suddenly, there was a rustle in the trees and a large herd of about one hundred deer came walking by the pond. They stopped for a drink and then continued on their pilgrimage. It was the perfect ending to a wonderful day. What a happy Thanksgiving!

The next day we had an appointment to meet with Dennis Kusy, a longtime local realtor referred to us by Chef Ross. He showed us ten properties, all up and down Highway 290 east of Fredericksburg. Finally, he showed us properties that bordered the Pedernales River. The Pedernales River is a tributary of the Colorado River given its name by the Spanish explorers in honor of the abundant flint rocks that cover the area.

It is one hundred six miles long and flows west to east through Hill Country all the way to Austin. When the river water is high, tubing down the river is popular on a hot summer day. People come from all over to hike, camp, and swim especially near Johnson City. In the fall and winter months, the state even stocks trout in the river. Pedernales means flint rocks in Spanish. The river passes right through President Johnson's Ranch. Shallow at spots, it reminded me of some of the wading streams back home in New York.

The first property he showed us was off of Highway 16 on the way to Willow City. The Oberhellmann winery was on that road. He even took us to the Kerrville area on Highway 16 not far from the

Kerrville Winery. We looked all over Gillespie, Kerr, Mason, and Llano counties. We really wanted to stay near Fredericksburg and finally settled on a beautiful piece of land off of Dusty Farm Lane.

"Look at the willow trees with the moss hanging!' I exclaimed to my wife. "Can you feel the breeze? I can hear the doves cooing in the trees."

Joanne smiled and took my hand. "You are in love," she said.

She was right. I fell in love with the property and the river. We bought fifteen-acres along the Pedernales - right in the heart of Texas Wine Country. It was part of a three-hundred-acre property that had been subdivided over the past thirty years.

Dennis had told us that the land was cleared by the original landowner, who raised Angus cows. "His original desire was to sell only to cattle ranchers who wished to raise high-end beef. He had a lucrative contract to sell his own high-end Angus to restaurants in Dallas, Houston, and Austin. When the restaurant business had a downward trend, many of those restaurants went out of business, so demand for his cows decreased. He started selling off parcels of his ranch to people who were interested in things other than cattle."

Dennis said the fifteen acres were a great opportunity to purchase cleared land with water on the back of the property. He then told me that my neighbors would be a cattle rancher and a retired pro-football player.

Chapter 5

One day while visiting with Ned, the wine steward at the downtown Fredericksburg HEB, he told me about Texas wines. Ned had an amazing wine department and the HEB was a fantastic grocery store. In New York we had extremely limited produce, fish, and meats. In this store, it seemed like there was everything.

Fredericksburg is a town of only eleven thousand people, but on the weekends more than five hundred bed and breakfasts are filled with visitors from all over the world. Its German charm is the host to more than two hundred festivals and events per year.

Ned suggested, "This is a new wine that I just got in. It is a Sagrantino Reserva from Messina Hof Winery." He continued, "They have a winery/tasting room on 290 east of town. You should visit them."

"We know. That is where we are staying – in one of their Manor Hauses. It is so charming. We stopped at their Messina Hof Harvest Green in Richmond, Texas, on our way here."

Ned continued, "There are over one hundred seventy wineries in the Hill Country now and there are tour buses that take you around. When you have time, you should see the Pioneer Museum and the Nimitz

Museum. They are excellent storytellers of local history."

Just then, Jim Kamas came into the store with associate Trevor Talan.

Ned introduced us, "Jim is a Texas viticultural pioneer and has been the horticulturalist in the area for many years. He is an associate professor and horticulturist for Texas A&M AgriLife Extension.

"Jim, this is Johnny Boone. He is new to the area and has bought acreage just outside of town. He and his wife moved here from New York."

Jim shook my hand, and I could feel the roughness in his hand of a man that was familiar with the soil.

Jim introduced me and Ned to Trevor, "This is Trevor Talan. He has recently taken Dr. McEachern's position as professor and extension horticulturist at Texas A&M University and is joining us in the extension office helping all grape growing regions of Texas."

Trevor shared, "Welcome to Texas. I was originally from Oklahoma. I got my degree in Texas working with vineyards and wineries in the High Plains. Recently, I have been collaborating with the growers and wineries in the Brazos Valley."

Jim added, "Trevor is known as our Sherlock of the Texas wine industry. He is very intuitive and able to figure out mysteries – not only in the vineyard but in life itself."

Trevor pointed to the diverse Texas wine selection in Ned's store and said, "Look at all these different varietals and diverse appellations on these labels. Texas just seems to have Spanish, Italian, Portuguese, and French grapes, plus many more. Tasting through these Texas wines is like tasting through Europe."

I was so impressed with their knowledge of grape growing in Texas. "I am really going to be enjoy all these different types of wines."

Jim said, "I received my horticulture degree and master's degree from Texas A&M and spent many years in New York at the Cornell University extension program. My job has evolved to advise peach and grape growers all over Texas."

John said, "You may know some of the wineries that we visited in the Finger Lakes……

Jim smiled, "Yes, I have visited them all."

"Trevor is in the Hill Country on a special project to learn what varieties grow best there."

"Yes, and I am particularly fascinated by the Sagrantino that Messina Hof was growing in Bryan, Fredericksburg, and the High Plains."

Trevor continued, "The grape is believed to be indigenous to Umbria, but it seems to be very adaptable. Jim has been a wealth of horticultural expertise for many decades. I hope to be able to continue his work."

I asked Trevor to tell me more about his background and his research.

Treavor shared, "After graduating college I received my master's degree in viticulture and was fortunate to join the team at Texas A&M University.

"So far my research has shown that Texas' diverse soil elevation and climate can support ninety-five percent of the world's varietals. Choosing the right grapes for the Hill Country is easy. French, Spanish, Italian, and Portugues grapes should do well. The two concerns are Pierces Disease and Cotton Root Rot. If you decide to grow grapes, I would be happy to help you."

Jim added, "My expertise is in Pierces Disease and Cotton Root Rot, two of the Hill Country's major limiting factors to expanding the wine industry here."

Jim asked me what I would do with my fifteen acres, "Have you thought about growing grapes?"

I told him no, but I was thinking about raising goats.

Jim laughed, "You do not look like a goat herder. Would you like to visit a new vineyard? There is one planted on Highway 16 just north of Kerrville."

I thought this would be a fantastic opportunity and followed them in my car.

The vineyard was owned by a Portuguese family that moved from Portugal due to the terrible drought that the area had been having. They were the Vadus family from the Douro Valley. Theirs' was the first vineyard in Texas planted exclusively with Portuguese varietals and were working with Jim and Trevor in their experimentation.

The Vaduses planted three acres each of Touriga National, Tinto Baraca, Tinto Cao, Tinto Roriz, and Tinto Franca. I was fascinated by the determination of the family and how well Jim and Trevor were collaborating with them. I was excited to meet the Vadus Family. The courage they must have had to journey all the way from Portugal and arrive in Texas! Imagine learning a new language, immigrating to a new country, and re-establishing a vineyard in a foreign land.

Julio and Maria Vadus both attended winemaking school in Lisbon, Portugal. Julio was kind enough to tell me all about his family, "Our Portuguese winery was called Vinhos Vadus. It was in Pinhao, Portugal. It consisted of twenty acres of steeply planted terraced vineyards.

"The Douro is not a forgiving land. Portugal has very traditional rules. Vineyards can only be irrigated in the first three years. So, when the great drought occurred, our vineyard, which was older than three years, died. We had no choice but to look elsewhere.

"When in college, Jim Kamas spoke to my class in Lisbon and inspired me to consider Texas. In Texas, irrigation is possible every year, and Texas is second only to California for wine tourism. Fredericksburg was the perfect place to relocate."

Julio introduced me to his twelve-year-old daughter, Esther, and ten-year-old son, Peter, "This is Mr. John Boone. He is new to Fredericksburg, too, and a friend of Jim and Trevor."

They politely said hello. I asked them how they liked Texas. They said in unison, "We love Texas! We have ponies and sheep." Julio said they had ponies and sheep in Portugal, too, and that it was a good way to help them transition. They loved and cared for their animals.

Julio reflected, "Portuguese varieties should do well in Texas. It will make our transition to Texas much easier."

Julio's wife Maria invited me to taste her Portuguese specialty Pastel de Nata. It is a custard tart. She was so generous to share her recipe with me.

Pastel de Nata

Dough:
    1 cup all-purpose flour
    ¼ teaspoon kosher salt
    ⅓ cup cold water
    1 stick unsalted butter, fully softened, divided

Sugar Syrup:
    ¾ cup white sugar
    ¼ cup water
    1 tablespoon Blanc du Bois wine
    1 cinnamon stick
    1 lemon, grated

Custard Base:
    ⅓ cup all-purpose flour
    ¼ teaspoon kosher salt
    1 ½ cups milk
    6 large egg yolks
    1 teaspoon vanilla extract

Directions:

1. Combine flour, salt, and cold water in a bowl. Mix with a wooden spoon until dough just comes together and pulls away from the sides of the bowl. Dough should be sticky; adjust with more flour or water.

2. Transfer dough onto a well-floured surface. Coat your hands in oil and knead for 1 to 2 minutes to form a round. Cover and let rest for 15 to 20 minutes.

3. Roll dough into a square about 1/8-inch-thick, dusting with flour as necessary; dough should still be sticky.

4. Spread 1/3 of the butter over $^2/_3$ of the square, leaving a 1/2-inch border. Fold the dough into thirds.

5. Turn dough and dust with flour. Flip and sprinkle more flour on top. Roll dough into a 1/8-inch-thick rectangle. Spread another 1/3 of the butter over 2/3 of the dough. Fold into thirds. Transfer onto a lined baking sheet and freeze until butter is slightly chilled, about 10 minutes.

6. Sprinkle dough with flour and roll into a square a little over 1/8-inch-thick. Spread remaining butter over the dough, leaving a 1- to 1 1/2-inch border on the top edge. Lightly moisten the unbuttered edge with water. Roll dough into a log. Dust with more flour. Seal with plastic wrap and refrigerate overnight.

7. Combine sugar, water, wine, cinnamon, and lemon zest in a pot. Boil over medium heat, without stirring, until syrup reaches 210 to 215 degrees. Remove from heat.

8. Preheat the oven to 500 degrees F. Grease a 12-cup muffin tin.

9. Whisk flour, salt, and cold milk together in a saucepan. Cook over medium heat, whisking constantly, until milk thickens, about 5 minutes. Remove from heat and let cool for at least 10 minutes.

10. Whisk egg yolks into the cooled milk. Add sugar syrup and vanilla extract. Mix until combined. Strain custard into a glass measuring cup.

11. Unwrap the dough and trim any uneven bits on the ends. Score log into 12 even pieces using a knife; cut through.

12. Line muffin cups at least 1/8 inch past the top. Fill each cup 3/4 of the way with custard.

13. Bake in the preheated oven until the pastry is browned and bubbly, and the tops start to blister and caramelize, about 12 minutes. Cool tarts briefly and serve warm.

Maria asked me, "John, can you bring your wife Joann over to the house so I could teach her good Portuguese cooking?"

"I know she would love that, Maria," I replied, "Next month I am taking Joann on a river cruise down the Douro."

In fact, Joann and I had planned a river cruise in Portugal with AmaWaterways. We were told the land is dramatically beautiful and that they had been making wine there since 2000 BC. AmaWaterways takes guests on cruises up and down the Douro visiting the Quintas. We were excited to learn about their terroir and taste their wines. We had been planning this trip for quite some time but this visit with the Vadus family made me even more determined to go.

As I left Jim, Trevor, and the Vadus family, I told Jim and Trevor that I would discuss the idea of planting a 5-acre vineyard with my wife. Jim told me to call him once I made up my mind and that he and Trevor would help me get started and include my vineyard in their project.

When I gave the recipe to Joann and mentioned Maria's invitation, she jumped at the opportunity. We set a dinner date. The ladies would cook together. I gathered my cruise information and itinerary and took it with us to see Maria and Julio.

Maria and Joann cooked together all day. The kitchen smelled amazing. Caldo Verde, Arroz de Pato, and Pastel de Nata were on the menu. Julio explained to me that this would be a traditional meal.

Over dinner, we talked about our future trip to Portugal. Julio seemed so excited about the opportunity to share his suggestions. He even offered to make arrangements with a distant cousin in Vinho Verde who was a Count. Count Joseph still maintained an ancient manor house and vineyard. Vinho Verde literally means green wine. The region consists of thousands of small growers in the very north of Portugal.

Julio offered, "Count Joseph could drive down to Porto to pick you up and take you to his vineyard and manor house."

"That would be wonderful," I eagerly accepted.

Dinner was wonderful, Joann had a new best friend in Maria, and I was dreaming of our time in Portugal.

Chapter 6

Our AmaWaterways Douro cruise was scheduled for next month, so Joann and I booked our cabins and started planning our pre-trip to Vinho Verde. Joann researched climates, luggage, and events. I researched transportation, restaurants, and wine. We developed quite a notebook of travel plans.

Count Joseph emailed us. "Dear Joann and John, my relative Julio Vadus has brought it to my attention that you will be traveling to Portugal. I hope you will visit us in Vinho Verde, and I insist that you stay as our guests at our manor house. I will pick you up at your hotel one or two days after you fly into Porto."

"Joann! Joann!" I shouted as I ran to the kitchen. "Count Joseph has invited us as his personal guests to the manor house!" Joann was beside herself with excitement. She called Maria and shared the good news.

Time passed quickly and before we knew it, the month was gone. We packed, got our plane tickets, and flew to Porto, Portugal. As we flew into Porto, the airplane approached the coastline layered in mystical, undulating clouds. Shadows of mountains peeked through the mist. Once we landed, we were driven through the mist to our hotel, PortoBay Flores.

What a magical arrival! The people were so nice. They reminded us of Texans. Porto Bay Flores is a lovely five-star hotel in the center of Porto. It is on the Rua das Flores, a beautiful pedestrian street in Porto. The hotel has a five-hundred-year history.

That evening, the hotel general manager, Luis Sante', hosted the wine and cheese reception. We talked about our journey to Portugal, our home in Texas, and our love of wine and antiques. His eyes sparkled as he offered to take us to an antique market in town the next morning. We were delighted.

After breakfast the next day, Joann and I met Luis in the lobby. Pointing to his car, he smiled and nodded that we should get in. At the antique market, Luis explained the types of antiques we would find and the prices to expect. I did not see anything of interest but some pottery tiles which are famous in Porto. Even some of the buildings were covered in hand painted tiles. Joann found a cute handheld mirror but decided not to get it. It was too expensive.

Disappointed that we had yet to find an item eye-catching enough to buy, Luis drove us to two other markets and an antique store. At one point when Luis stepped away from us, I told Joann, "He seems determined to shop until we find something. Let's look harder for something to buy."

Our last stop was after dark at an antique shop that appeared to be open just for us.

"Luis must have made arrangements for the owner to wait for us," I told Joann. As we looked around, we found a plate with a painting of a man making wine barrels. Luis explained, "The wine barrel man is called a Cooper. They make by hand the barrels in which wine was stored and transported."

"What is the price?" I asked sheepishly since nothing had price tags. Luis asked the merchant for me.

"He says $35," responded Luis. "Would you like it?"

"Yes," I said as I handed him the money. The store owner wrapped it nicely for safe travel. I thought to myself that it would make a nice gift for the Vadus family.

When we got back to the hotel, Luis invited us for a glass of wine. He gave us pointers on what to see in Porto the next day. "The city of Porto is a blend of old and new. The historic quarter, a UNESCO World Heritage Site, and the beautiful Portuguese blue and white tile panels depicting scenes from Portuguese history are some key attractions you won't want to miss. You'll also want to enjoy a tasting of Port, Portugal's most renowned contribution to the world of wine."

I told Luis that we were heading to Vinho Verde to stay with the Count Joseph. His eyes got big, and he said, "You must see the vineyards and the chapel. A manor house like that from the 7th or 8th century was the center of activity for all who lived in the area. It is quite historic!"

As we left to retire for the night, Luis handed Joann a small satin bag and said, "Open this when you get back to your room. It has been a pleasure to spend the day with you both and to get to know you. Best wishes on your adventures."

Once back in our room, Joann pulled open the satin bag to find the lovely handheld mirror she had seen earlier in the day but rejected as too expensive. "How thoughtful," she said, "Luis must have seen me looking at this and bought it for me."

It brought a tear to her eye. She wrote a thank you note addressed to Luis and left it in our room when we checked out. We never saw Luis again, but each time we see the mirror or think of Porto, we think of him.

Chapter 7

Count Joseph picked us up at the hotel. We left our luggage at PortoBay Flores and took a small overnight bag on this part of the trip. Luis told us he would help us get our luggage to the AmaWaterways ship upon our return.

The drive to Vinho Verde reflected the name – green. Vinho Verde means green wine and the region is known for its dry, crisp white wines that have a green tint in the color. The land was hilly and green with wildflowers along the roadside.

Joann commented, "I thought Texas had the most wildflowers, but this area can compete. It is so beautiful and colorful!"

As we drove through the gates of the manor and over a bridge spanning a moat, a majestic, ancient, gray stone building appeared beyond the rows of blooming apple trees and a grape-covered arbor outlining the trail around the vineyard.

Remains of fortress walls now hidden behind trailing ivy spoke to the peace this region has enjoyed for so many generations.

The Count made us feel like we were family. He offered, "Let me give you a tour of the manor". We followed and learned so much history.

He shared, "Did you know that this northwestern part of Portugal has been making wine at least two thousand years? They were making wine in this green belt region before the Romans came there. The name Vinho Verde means green wine."

The Manor house sat at the top of a hillside vineyard overlooking a river. The grounds were perfectly manicured. Tall ancient trees formed a backdrop for the time-patinaed house which seemed to have such a sense of place there.

Count Joseph told us, "My family has lived here for seven hundred years. During the Middle Ages, the manor house was deeded to the head of my family and he was made "lord" by the king. The lord lived there and ruled over a feudal estate that cared for the surrounding village and villagers. There are twenty-five rooms to accommodate everyone who worked here."

We entered a two-story solid chestnut wood door that was at least three inches thick. To the right was a great hall with an elaborately hand painted ceiling mural depicting a war scene surrounded by angels. There the lord held court and banquet feasts for the locals as well as served communal meals for the tenants who worked on the estate.

Finally, he showed us our room. It overlooked the valley and vineyards. The walls were two feet thick. As we looked out the window, I thought about how many people before me had looked out this same window over this same valley and vineyards. It was a great reminder that we are here for such a brief time and only a small part of this world's history.

Bedtime was another adventure. A three-step ladder was required just to climb into the bed. The manor house was not heated so the night was cold. They provided a pile of five quilts and extra blankets to keep us warm.

Joann snuggled and whispered, "I feel like the Princess and the Pea – so many mattresses and so comfortable! You are my prince." We giggled. I did feel like royalty.

Count Joseph met us for breakfast and took us to the vineyards and winery. He pointed to the vineyards and said, "They are so symmetrical and graceful. The straight rows and cascading branches create a comforting since of uniformity and stability."

At the end of each row was what looked like concrete posts instead of the wood posts I had seen in Texas. The Count shared, "These are granite posts. It is a tradition here to make them out of granite. They last longer and are stronger."

I inquired about what grape varieties he grew. He said, "The most well-known are Alvarinho and Loureiro. I made a mental note to ask Trevor about these grapes.

Joann smiled at me and said, "Are you beginning to think like a grape farmer?"

As we walked under the grape covered arbors along the vineyard trail, we came upon a large round wooden door which led into a cave carved into the mountainside. It led to the winery which was under the manor house.

Count Joseph said, "The large round door was made from the base of an original wooden fermentation tank. The cave environment provides natural cooling, so we need no refrigeration. Let's taste some wine."

Count Joseph explained, "This wine is a DOC ("Denominação de Origem Controlada" or Denomination of Controlled Origin) which means that this region is a protected region that can only produce these varieties. It is usually cheaper than other wines, but still delicious. We eat a lot of seafood. It is the perfect wine with cod."

I asked Count Joseph why cod was so dominant in Portuguese cuisine, "Is codfish abundant in the waters off Portugal? I have seen it on menus for breakfast, lunch, and dinner."

He laughed, "The cod comes from Norway. In the Middle Ages the Portuguese sold salt to Norway and Norway sold cod to Portugal. Salted cod became a staple in the Portuguese cuisine."

Our last stop was the chapel Julio had told us about. It was a small building off the manor house. Though plain on the outside, the doors opened into a room with ceramic tiled walls featuring hand painted scenes of life in the 8th century. The massive marble altar was supported and surrounded by large-hand carved columns covered in grapes.

Joann and I both gasped as we walked into the chapel. There in front of us was the most elaborately carved altar we had ever seen.

Joann exclaimed, "How beautiful! Is this hand carved? The entire altar is covered in grapes and grapevines with angels."

Count Joseph smiled, "Yes, this is the original altar built six hundred years ago. The wood is hand carved and depicts the celebration of the blessing of harvest. Do you see the wording carved into the front of the altar?"

We both nodded, speechless to find words to describe the magnificence of what was before us.

He continued, "The carving is John 15:8 'This is to my Father's glory, that you bear much fruit, showing yourselves to be my disciples.' This is the foundation of our core values."

Count Joseph continued, "The chapel is always open for the family and villagers. Everyone in this area is baptized and married in this chapel."

I asked, "Why were ceramic tiles so popular on the outside surfaces of buildings in Portugal?"

He responded, "Manuel I, the reigning King of Portugal, was so impressed by ceramic tiles made in Sevilla, Spain, that he started decorating all of his palace walls with them. They were not only beautiful, but they also protected the walls from dampness and low temperatures."

As we said goodbye to our host, we presented him with some Texas pecan pie mix we had brought from home.

Chapter 8

On the way back to Porto, Joann and I talked about all we had seen and learned with Count Joseph.

"Isn't it amazing to think that people have lived and made wine here for so many centuries?" Joann asked, "I can't wait to learn more along the Douro."

The streets of Porto were steep and winding. Many were cobblestone. Our driver took us past so many buildings covered in the beautiful tiles. We made a note to look for tiles to take home.

As we drove along the Douro River, Joann noticed the port houses on the hill across the waters. "Look," she said, "Grahams, Sandeman, so many port houses. And look at the river! There is a boat with barrels on it."

The driver responded, "Those are Rabelo boats. They transport the Port wine barrels from the wineries upriver to these cellars you see on the river in Vila Nova de Gaia."

We could see a Gondola from the top of the hill gliding down to the Port houses below. There seemed to be several Rabelo boats parked there.

The driver anticipated my question, "Those boats are like living museums. They are no longer used to move wine barrels except on special holidays."

I asked, "How is the wine moved today?"

The driver answered, "About twenty-five years ago, they began to ship the wines via train and then later by truck. The wine is aged in the barrels in Porto."

That afternoon we boarded our AmaWaterways boat in Porto. Luis had already delivered our luggage.

Joann looked at me excitedly and said, "I think I could get use to this lifestyle."

The first impression of the river was how steep and terraced the land was. The vineyards were planted on the terraces, and the soil looked like very thin layers of slate. They called it Schist. It is not as hard as slate and is more granular in texture. This causes it to slough off with erosion. Many vineyards had bulldozers repairing the terraces.

Joann pointed to a sunny area and said, "Look Johnny, when the sun hits the rocks just right they glimmer browns, greens, and grays. It looks like an earthtone Moire' water pattern impressed in the soil."

In Regua we visited the Baroque-style Mateus Palace and gardens. That was a special place for us because of Mateus Rose'.

"Joann, do you remember where we shared our first wine?"

"Of course, I do! We were in school in New York. It was our first official date. You took me to Carmine's family Italian restaurant in Manhattan. I had my first taste of wine. It was Mateus Rose', a very popular rose' in a strange bottle made in Portugal. How romantic that you remembered," she smiled.

The ship came to a narrow gorge that looked like we might not make it through. Joann and I went to the bow to see how close it would come. It seemed like we could reach over the edge of the boat and touch the rocky cavern wall.

The Captain did a great job. Then we went through a lock. It was a one hundred eighty-five feet tall three-sided concrete wall we approached. The ship eased into the tight three-sided box. The walls of the lock were so close we could touch them from the bow. The back of the lock closed. We were in the bottom of a one hundred eighty-five-foot-deep concrete box.

Joann looked concerned and grabbed my hand. I comforted her, "Look at me. Do you feel the mist on your face? It feels so cool. Look at the water rising. The ship is floating on the water as it rises in the lock."

Suddenly, water began to flow into the lock. The ship slowly rose to the level of the river above.

Then in Pinhao we had our first official Port wine tasting and saw the most amazing train station covered in tiles depicting the grape harvest and country life. The tiles are hand painted by local artists.

At Dao Port house in Pinhao, we got a tour of the property and had red and white wines paired with foods as we sat overlooking the Douro River and watched the sunlight dance through the old olive tree branches.

The buildings were full of high beam ceilings and beautiful wooden doors that looked like they had been there three hundred years. It was a lovely, quaint, small city where everyone knew each other.

In Barca d'Alva, we visited the medieval Castelo Rodrigo, which had a Gothic castle. I love castles! As a child, I used to pretend to be the king of the castle and had my knights at a round table. This castle did not have a round table, but was amazing, nonetheless.

AmaWaterways does such an excellent job of featuring the cuisine of the region. We got to taste local traditional specialties, such as Bola de Lamego, bread filled with smoked ham; Presunto, a type of Portuguese dry-cured ham; and Espumante, a Portuguese sparkling wine.

The wine hosts onboard shared that the Phoenicians started planting in the more northern regions of Portugal. Later, the Romans spread grape growing and winemaking all over the area.

They told us that Portuguese wine became very popular in England in the 12th century AD. In 1386, England and Portugal signed the Treaty of Windsor formalizing trade between both countries.

During the American Revolution, England stopped buying French wine and shifted to purchasing Portuguese wines. France was helping the colonies, so England closed the door to French imports.

At first, Portugal was known for Port wine, but now their white, red, and rose' table wines have become very popular around the world. Due to the warming of the environment, Portuguese grape varieties have become desirable in other wine growing regions. We were surprised to learn that the climate in Portugal, especially in the Douro Valley, is very similar to the Texas Hill Country climate. It gave us much more appreciation for what the Vaduses were doing.

As our time aboard ended back in Porto, we reflected on the lifestyle there. Local foods are harvested fresh from the gardens. The wines are local. Families dine together at the table each evening. It is a priority. Joann and I wanted that lifestyle in Texas. Grape growing could be our connection to that lifestyle.

Chapter 9

On the flight home, I could not stop thinking about all that we had seen in Portugal. Images of our own magical vineyard in Fredericksburg filled my mind. Back in Texas, I met with Jim Kamas and Trevor Talan and shared with him all that we had learned in Portugal. I was ready to plant Portuguese grapes.

I asked Trevor what he thought about it.

He told me that no one was growing the Vinho Verde varieties in Texas, "I am afraid the humidity might be too much. You could have disease problems. Dry climates like the High Plains can grow tight cluster varietals. If you want to plant something new, stick with the Sagrantino. I think you will have more luck."

Our land borders the Pedernales River. The riverbanks were not as tall and majestic as those we had seen on the Douro, but they were just as beautiful in a different rustic Texas way. I told Joann that I was excited that our Boone family from New York was going into the wine grape growing business in the Texas Hill Country.

She giggled and ran to get a bottle of wine. We toasted this new adventure. She said, "Johnny Boone, I think you are crazy, but after being married to you for twenty years, we may as well go crazy together."

I called Jim and Trevor, and they came out to visit our land. It is a lovely five-acre plot that has sandy loam soil close to the Pedernales river. We took soil samples and Trevor sent them off to the Texas A&M soil laboratory. Trevor took water samples from the old well that was drilled by the original settler on the property. Two weeks later, Trevor told me that everything looked good.

Jim, Trevor, and I met at the land and talked about what to plant where and how. I shared with them what Ned had said about Sagrantino Reserva at Messina Hof.

Trevor said, "Well then, let's share a bottle while we make these plans." I called Joann and she brought wine and glasses.

While Trevor drew out a vineyard plan for our land, I contacted Inland Desert Nursery in Washington State and ordered our grapevines. Trevor reached out to

Bill's Vineyard Services to plant the grapes next spring.

Trevor called his girlfriend, Lulu, to tell her about the new vineyard and suggested she come to help plant. She said, "Absolutely! I would love to help."

"What type of trellis do you want to use, John?" asked Trevor. "Trellis systems are very important."

I immediately said I wanted granite posts like I had seen in Portugal. Trevor said that they may be hard to find, and that I might have to have them custom-made.

I researched Sagrantino vineyards and found that many in Umbria, the birthplace of the grape, were head trained. They looked like a bush in Umbria. That meant no trellis, which would save money, but required more labor to train. "I think it would be the second head trained vineyard in the Hill Country," I remarked.

Jim confirmed, "Messina Hof was the first head trained vineyard."

Trevor said, "Even with head training, you will need some sort of trellis. Sagrantino is a very vigorous vine that needs support. It will take three years before you get a crop."

Fortunately, granite is a common rock found in the Hill Country. I remembered a granite supplier next to Messina Hof Hill Country on Highway 290 so I called them. Schulmack Granite was very accommodating and excited about the challenge to do something new and different.

Plans were done and everything was ordered. I could not wait to get started.

Joann and I wanted to get to know our neighbors. The neighbor to the south was an old, retired builder named Johan Nessel who ran Simmental cattle. They are a Swiss breed from Bern. Our neighbor's family, the Nessel Family, were originally from Switzerland.

Joann and I went to their home and knocked on the door. Through the glass, there was a shadow of a man ambling toward the door. He slowly opened the door and stood there looking at us.

"Hello," we said, "We are John and Joann Boone, your new neighbors."

"Hello," he said, "would you like to come in?" We thanked him for his invitation and walked inside. The house was filled with photos of cows. Even his chairs were sturdy oak covered in cowhides. Longhorns decorated the wall over the fireplace and around the living room. In the dining room there was a large rough-hewn table made of cedar planks. Vintage ranch tools adorned the walls. A coiled lasso framed a set of spurs hanging on the hat rack with many work hats. It was like walking straight into a western movie set.

He led us to his back patio, where he had rocking chairs. We all sat there looking toward the new vineyard location.

I asked Johan about his family. He shared that the Nessel family immigrated from Bern, Switzerland, when Europe was experiencing mad cow disease. They, along with six other families from Switzerland, arrived in Fredericksburg and soon became pillars of the community.

Johan was a big, scraping man. He had some of the largest and calloused hands I had ever seen. His broad shoulders reflected his years of hard work, and rosy nose the many cases of beer he had enjoyed.

Johan introduced us to his son, Ivan. Ivan was just the opposite of Johan. He was slight in build and short in stature.

"Tell us about yourself, Ivan."

"I attended Rice University and was a construction engineer by trade. I took Johan's construction company into commercial construction as well as residential."

Ivan told us he was happy the Boone family had moved in next door. "It makes me feel better to know my father has a neighbor to help keep an eye on him. I tried to get Johan to sell off the Simmental cattle. I was afraid he would get hurt caring for them. Plus, his cows always seemed more important to him than my children, Johan's grandchildren. I want Dad to be less passionate about the cows and be more involved with his grandchildren. It is time for him to be a grandfather."

That was an awkward moment. Ivan had obviously been thinking about this for a long time. I suggested that Joann and I could get him involved in some activity other than his cows.

"Johan enjoyed hunting and fishing. Often, I invited him to come with me fishing and hunting, but Johan was always busy with his cows. He is obsessed. He even missed Thanksgiving dinner because one of his cows was going to have a calf. When the calf died Johan was depressed for weeks."

I thought it was so strange for a man to be more obsessed about his cows than his family. There had to be more to the story.

Chapter 10

"Ivan, something must have happened that caused Johan to live like this. What happened?" I asked.

Ivan looked at me and then out toward the horizon. He thoughtfully paused and said, "I had a sister. She was my father's joy. She loved to help him with the cows ever since she was old enough to walk. Every morning and every evening, Johan took her little hand and together they walked to the barn to milk the cows. She danced and sang as they walked. Johan smiled and laughed as he was entertained by my sister's energetic joy.

"One day, my sister was up early and waiting for our father. She hoped to surprise him in the barn, so she went ahead. She tried to climb a wall to fetch the milk pail and fell, hitting her head on a wooden trough. By the time Father got there, she was dead. He never forgave himself. The cows are his connection to the daughter he lost."

We sat there in silence for a few moments. Ivan spoke, "My mother was a teacher and loving mom. She and my dad were close. We were all excited about my new baby sister coming. Mother died in childbirth.

That is why my sister was so precious to dad. She was the perfect likeness to my mom, blond hair, blue eyes, and a smile as big as the sun. He saw the spirit of mom in her."

I put my arm around Ivan as though he was my son. We just stood there for a few minutes.

"Thank you for listening and caring," said Ivan.

My heart hurt for him. I replied, "It must have been difficult losing your mom, your sister, and in a way, your father, too."

Ivan reminisced, "Dad tried to be strong and tried to be father and mother to me. But he seemed so sad, so aloof, so angry all the time. I tried to be good and help around the house, but nothing I did was ever good enough. Dad just kept drinking whiskey and more beer, sitting on his porch, and caring for his cows. It is what it is. I couldn't do anything about it." He shook my hand and walked away.

Joann and I talked about how we could include Ivan and his family in ours. I realized I had to be very careful around Johan and his cows. They could spell trouble for the Boone family vineyards.

I reached out to Johan for advice on preparing our land for the vineyard, thinking that it would make him feel more involved. Johan had not seemed too excited about me and Joann moving into the neighborhood.

When I asked him about the land prep he told me, "I have lived on this property my entire life. I have built many homes in the Hill Country and retired five years ago. My son Ivan took over the construction business. I should have gotten that fifteen acres you bought. The owner rejected my offer. Before I knew it, the land was sold to the Boones."

I think he owned his property for so many years he forgot how much the land prices had gone up in value. I wound up paying twice as much for those fifteen acres than Johan was willing to pay.

Johan had fifty cows and his fences were old. Occasionally, I would see one of his cows wander onto our land. Our dog, Prince, would help to drive the cow back to Johan's property.

I offered to go in halves to put in a new fence because I was afraid his cows would get into my new vineyard once it was planted.

Johan bristled, "My fences are just fine. They have been there for many years and there is no reason to spend good money on a new fence just because you are putting in a vineyard. I don't think my cows would like your grapes anyway."

This was no way to start a new relationship with my neighbor to the south. I told him that we could talk about it again after I put in the vineyard. Cattle prices were down, so I thought Johan was not able to buy a new fence. I even considered paying for the new fence entirely, but I did not think Johan would go for it.

Chapter 11

My neighbors to the north were Mary and Manny Effor. I called to say hello. Mary answered, "Howdy, this is Mary." I introduced myself and invited myself to come by to say hello. She graciously invited me to meet them.

I rang the doorbell. Suddenly, there was a dog loudly barking and running around inside. Then there was a crash against the front door. I stepped back considering what might happen when the door opened. A man and woman were shouting "Sonny, no!" inside. The door opened. A woman was holding the dog's collar.

She gathered her composure and introduced herself, "Hi, I am Mary, and this is our dog, Sonny. Sonny is part Pitbull, part boxer rescue dog. My husband really wanted a boxer and absolutely loves his Sonny. But Sonny is very protective and is not very hospitable."

As I entered their home, I saw football photos everywhere. The players in the photos looked huge, muscular, and fearless.

I asked, "What is your interest in football?"

I watched Sonny out of the corner of my eye. Each time I looked toward him, he growled. It became a bit of a game.

Mary pulled on Sonny's collar and responded, "We met when I was a cheerleader for Miami. It was love at first sight. My husband Manny is a retired footballer. Manny played for Dallas as a nose guard for twelve years."

She paused and shared, "He sustained many injuries and is in the early stages of dementia. We bought our land about five years before you bought yours. It is a place for us to get away and a place for healing."

She introduced me to Manny. I was shocked. Before me was a frail man hunched over a TV tray. He looked nothing like the pictures on the walls. Manny talked about his playing days like they were yesterday. I shook Manny's hand, "I am a Dallas fan."

He smiled and welcomed me to the area. I asked how he and Mary met. There was a long uncomfortable pause while he collected his thoughts. My impulse was to say something to fill the air, but I looked at Mary, who was patiently looking at Manny awaiting his response.

"Dallas was playing in Miami. The Miami cheerleaders came running out and there she was. She was a fantastic cheerleader with a big smile." He grinned sheepishly as he said, "She was so cute with her flowing blond hair, sparkling blue eyes, and great legs. How could I resist? I knew that I wanted to get to know her. Our plane home to Dallas did not leave until the next morning."

Mary laughed and blushed as she shared, "I had never dated a football player. Manny waited for me after the game. I thought he was so handsome. When he asked me to go with him to get a bite to eat, I quickly accepted."

Mary shared, "Manny grew up in Tenafly, New Jersey. His dad was a scout for the New York Giants. He did not want Manny to play high school football because he was saving Manny for a college football scholarship at Miami University. He felt the Miami football program provided the best path to the pros. "Manny's dad got his wishes except Dallas drafted Manny before the Giants could. That was his dad's one regret." She smiled and looked lovingly at her husband.

"Manny was 6'1" and weighed 220 pounds when he graduated from Tenafly High School. His dad managed his high school football career so that he would not be injured. He did not play on kick-offs, and if Tenafly were way ahead or behind in the fourth period the coach would sit him out. Manny even sat out most of the preseason.

"When Manny arrived at Miami University, he had to fight for his starting position on the football team. He was small compared to the other Miami linemen but blocked and tackled with vengeance.

"In the third game of his freshman year against Texas A&M, Manny was knocked out cold. He left the field on a stretcher and was in the hospital overnight. They said he had a concussion and released him.

Now we know that they treat concussions much more aggressively than they did then. The injured players were not even medically followed for symptoms. Change in behavior was chalked up to the fact that they were aggressive ex-football players. Today they have a concussion protocol. The player is kept out of the game until he can pass the concussion protocol tests.

After that, Manny's father had a specially padded helmet made for him. In Manny's sophomore and junior years, he had three other concussions. Each time, they put him back in the game.

Despite all this, he still made all-conference in his junior year. He was so aggressive. He fearlessly blocked opponents much larger than himself.

"In Manny's senior year, he was the third lineman picked in the National Football League draft. Although Manny's dad wanted him to be drafted by the New York Giants, the Giants did not have an early draft number. Dallas had an early number and they gobbled him up. Dallas loved Manny's aggressiveness. They told him they were going to groom him for the center.

Manny arrived at training camp and his outgoing personality at once made him a very popular member of the team. He had three more concussions in his twelve-year career."

I felt bad that I loved football so much. Looking at Manny made me think of what the ancient Roman gladiators had to do. Football captivates millions of fans. Players are admired as gods, especially America's team, the Dallas Cowboys. Manny was a star.

Mary reflected, "While Manny was playing, he would complain of headaches, especially after a massive collision on the field. Sometimes he had difficulty sleeping but chalked it up to pregame jitters. The gentle giant I had first met at Miami became an emotional man that flies off the handle and yells at me. Even my Hallmark movies caused him to be more emotionally affected than me. He became a different person.

"Manny was an all-pro for six of his twelve years in the NFL and retired from Dallas after a severe knee injury. Manny's dad got to see him retire. Unfortunately, the year after Manny retired, his dad died of a heart attack. Manny was devastated. He realized how much his dad had helped to guide his football career."

Mary shared, "the Dallas team doctor told me that Manny's many concussions would someday manifest itself as dementia. It was just a matter of time. I knew

Manny would need to be where he would be supported by a community and be celebrated. Fredericksburg was just that community.

Chapter 12

"When we moved into Fredericksburg, you would have thought the president had arrived," she continued, "Manny would walk on Main Street wearing his Superbowl rings and sign autographs. He loved being the Grand Marshall of the 4th of July parade."

Joann and I had heard that people would bring their pickup trucks to Main Street the night before the parade and park them in their favorite spots. No spots were available the morning of the parade. The residents put lawn chairs in their pickup beds and brought picnics, ice chests, and patriotic decorations for their trucks.

Mary continued, "Manny would go down to Sonja's Bakery on Main Street and hold court talking to visitors about his glory days while playing for Dallas. He would sign autographs.

"Manny even authored a book called <u>In the Huddle,</u> an inside look at what happened in the locker room during Manny's career at Dallas. Some of Manny's teammates were truly angry with him. In the book he revealed some of his teammates' infidelities and romantic escapades. Some of these revelations resulted in divorces. A few of his teammates even threatened harm to Manny and our family. I warned him to leave those stories out of the book, but Manny wanted to 'come clean'. Many rumors had been circulating and Manny just wanted to be honest."

I told her that I thought it was brave of him, but also a bit reckless. She agreed. "He is aggressive and passionate about everything. The older he gets, the more hostile and defensive he becomes."

One of the rumors around town was that Johnny P., an offensive tackle named in Manny's book, confronted Manny at a book signing. Johnny walked up to Manny and asked him to step outside and fight. When Manny told him to get lost, Johnny P jumped across the table and tried to tackle Manny. Manny ducked and clocked Johnny P. Johnny slumped to the ground. The customers in the store gasped and ran outside. Police had to be called. Someone could have been killed.

"After that incident threatening letters from Johnny P started coming." She seemed concerned, "Manny even got a license to carry a sidearm to protect himself. His mental status and judgement are worsening, and I am worried that Manny's impulsive nature could explode and cause him to do harm to himself or another.

"Johnny P. played alongside Manny in Dallas. He was from Florida State. Johnny was Manny's back up lineman. Johnny and Manny never got along. Johnny was smaller and less aggressive than Manny. When Manny would get injured, Johnny substituted. Johnny was the clown in the locker room and played tricks on Manny, Manny was a very serious professional and did not take kindly to these childish pranks.

"Johnny once hid Manny's helmet in the empty whirlpool just before game time. Manny went berserk. Johnny waited until five minutes before introduction to tell Manny where his helmet was.

"Manny raced to the whirlpool, grabbed his helmet, and ran out on the field. Johnny thought it was so funny. He was the guy responsible for ending Manny's career.

"The Cowboys were practicing and had an intersquad game at the end of Manny's twelfth season in the league. Johnny was lined up on Manny. Manny pulled to lead the blocking. As Manny was set to make a block on the defensive end, Johnny cross-blocked

Manny just above his knee. Manny's cruciate ligament popped, ending his season. Manny never recovered. His career ended with a dirty block on what was supposed to be light contact practice day.

"Manny never forgave Johnny When Manny wrote his book, Johnny locker room antics were in Manny's first chapter. '...*Johnny P. used to brag in the locker room how many women he had slept with before and after the away games*', he wrote."

Mary shook her head, "God tells us vengeance is the Lord's. Johnny thought that by removing Manny from the lineup, he would be playing full-time. Instead, the Cowboys traded Johnny to Washington, who was in last place, and his jealous Sicilian wife used Manny's book in a divorce proceeding against Johnny."

"Manny's personality was changing. He was not his jovial self. His stories were becoming dark. He even argued with fans that were not Dallas supporters. One day, he had a fist fight with a New York Giants fan right in front of the bakery. Thank God the Fredericksburg police loved Manny and broke up the fight. They gave Manny and the Giants fan a warning. No one was arrested."

Mary made many friends and even got involved with grief counseling in her church to help prepare herself for the future.

I looked at Manny as a tragic hero. Manny smiled at me. He looked like a man that had tasted glory but had a future of darkness and isolation.

Mary said, "Manny enjoys working in the garden except when the cows get in and eat everything. Then he gets very upset. The cattle break through the fence and wander into our garden. They eat all the leaves off the lettuce, tomatoes, and eggplant.

"We checked the ear tag on the cattle, and they belonged to Johan our neighbor to the south. We told Johan but got no response. Manny even called Sheriff Bartow who came out and escorted the cows back to Johan and asked him to fix his fence. I think he has lived out here alone so long that he is angry about all his new neighbors."

Tensions were developing along the Pedernales River due to Johan's stubbornness concerning his fence and his cows.

Since Manny loved to garden, I invited him to help me in the vineyard as my assistant vineyard manager. Manny seemed delighted. It was nice to see his excitement, but I was concerned about his judgement and impulsive nature. I am sure it is hard to be an aggressive all-pro lineman for twelve years and not have an aggressive nature.

To be as supportive as possible to Manny as my assistant vineyard manager, I wanted to know more about dementia caused by repeated traumatic brain injuries resulting from concussions. I began researching. The symptoms include memory loss and confused thinking, changes in personality and aggressive behavior. I decided Manny and I would work together and play together so that we could maintain the friendliest of relations.

Chapter 13

Joann was waiting for me with a glass of wine and a kiss. "How was your day? Tell me all about it."

We sat, sipped, and shared stories from each other's day. I love talking with her because she is such an attentive listener and laughs at my jokes and stories. It was the first thing that attracted me to her.

We were both in college at the same time. I was at Columbia; she was at NYU. When we had dinner, she would laugh so spontaneously at my jokes. She made every day a celebration.

Joann's dad was a Navy captain stationed at Oakland Naval Hospital. When he retired they moved to Westchester.

Joann told me, "Oakland Naval Hospital 'Oak Knoll' is a country club converted into a medical complex with the growing number of wounded soldiers returning from Vietnam. When dad retired from the Navy, we moved to Westchester, New York, where he worked at the Burke Rehabilitation Center."

When she lived in Oakland, her family would take trips to wineries in Napa and Sonoma. She did not taste because she was too young, but she loved the experience.

Joann was the one that talked me into going to the Finger Lake wineries for tastings. In California, she took me to wineries that her family had visited and tasted wine at wineries in Napa and Sonoma where she had been with her dad. The officers club would set up wine tastings in California Wine Country.

As we sat on our patio and sipped a Messina Hof Sagrantino she had purchased at the winery, she said, "You were so sweet to invite Manny to help you with the vineyard. That is so like you."

I told her of my concern about Manny's health. She smiled and said, "The Lord will guide you in this. You are doing a good work."

I told her, "I went down to the Kubota dealer and bought a narrow tractor with an air-conditioned cab. I also bought a disc, a sprayer, and a front-end loader. Then I went crazy and got a Jaco Air Blaster with a one-hundred-gallon tank."

Her eyes sparkled as she laughed, "Johnny Boone, you are so excited about planting a vineyard. I see the joy in your heart. It is a lot of money. Do you think the bank will give us the loan?"

She did not want to use up all our savings. I understood, especially after we had just committed to a mortgage on the land.

I made an appointment to visit with the loan officer at the Happy Bank of Fredericksburg. The loan officer, Mervin Penny, was referred to me by Johan's son Ivan. He told me that Mervin would fix me up. Ivan said, "Mervin is a good Christian man who will take care of you."

I went to the bank, presented my business plan, and asked for a five-year loan totaling $200,000.00. Mervin asked me why I wanted to grow grapes. I told him about our trip to Portugal and that I had a dream.

"In the dream a bright light appeared, and a faint voice came from the bright light. The voice said, 'Your destiny is to feed the world with exceptional wine.' When I awoke, there was a glass of red wine sitting on my bedside table. So, I knew the Lord had approved our venture."

Mervin's eyes teared up when he heard the dream. He shook my hand, wished me well, and approved the $200,000.00 loan on the spot. I did not even have to put up any collateral!

The drive home was like a blur. I rolled down the windows and turned up the radio. The song that was playing was about miracles. I sang it loud – my life was a miracle.

"Joann!" I yelled as I ran into the house. She smiled and hugged me, "You got the loan?"

"Yes! And I did not have to show any assets. It seemed the Lord paved the way for our loan approval and Mervin merely provided the money. Who has heard of a loan presentation like that? It was crazy! Now, we need to produce a crop within five years so we can start paying off the loan or even pay off the whole thing."

I jumped out of bed the next day and started discing five acres. I disced north and south, then east and west. Finally, I disced diagonally both ways. We arranged to start planting after the supplies and vines arrived in four to five weeks.

All the supplies arrived a month later. I called Jim and Trevor to plan a planting day. We arranged to start in a week.

Trevor said he would bring his girlfriend, Lulu. He shared with me that he met Lulu in the Brazos Bottom, and he wanted her to share the experience. "She is such a happy person, John. She reminds me of Joann. You will love her."

I could tell that Trevor was quite taken with Lulu and I asked him to tell me more. I could even tell over the phone that his eyes lit up when he spoke of her. He was delighted to tell me about Lulu, "Her eyes are like the color of warm honey. She has a radiant smile that lights up any room she enters. She has an aura of charm that draws people to her and a gentle and caring soul. She makes everyone around her feel valued and necessary.

"Her grace and elegance are like a ballet dancer. Her hair is flowing and cascading down her back like a gentle waterfall. She has a captivating and effortless personality.

"Beyond her physical beauty, she is intelligent and engaging with a childlike curiosity and eagerness to learn new things.

"Her laugh is contagious, and her sense of humor is playful and endearing. Lulu is a winner. Her life has been very challenging, and she has overcome each challenge set before her."

I said that it sounded like Lulu was a miracle for him and I appreciated that she is willing to help.

Trevor responded, "That is why I am so convinced that she will love meeting you and Joann and being part of the planting of your vineyard."

I looked at Trevor and said, "Wow, Trevor, you are definitely smitten over Lulu. You need to hold on to her. She sounds like a keeper."

Trevor laughed sheepishly and shared, "Our first encounter was totally by chance. It had to be a GodThing! I heard her laugh across a vineyard. Someone introduced us. She was so easy to talk to. She even taught me how to dance.

"I felt like I had always known her. We share so many common interests." He paused and added quietly, "What started as a friendship feels like it is turning into something much more."

Chapter 14

On the day of planting, everyone arrived just after sunrise. Trevor brought Lulu and introduced her. Joann greeted Lulu warmly, "It is so nice to meet you. Welcome to Hill Country and thank you so much for helping us start our dream."

Lulu seemed quite touched and gave Joann a hug. Trevor was right. They were so much alike. I suggested they work together.

Manny, Jim, Trevor, and I laid out the vineyard rows east to west. We tied knots in the rope every four feet and laid out a knotted rope along each row. Sagrantino is an aggressive grape, so I wanted to leave enough room between them for air circulation and the ability to get in between the plants to work them. A head trained vine looks a bit like a miniature weeping willow with the branches of the vine draping toward the ground.

After the knotted ropes were placed eight feet apart to give us enough room to run our equipment between the rows, Manny, Jim, and Trevor dug a hole at each knot. Then, Joann and Lulu laid out our drip irrigation along the same rows.

Lulu said, "Where is the music? We need music to work by." Joann thought that was a good idea and went to get a speaker. She set it up on the porch and set the volume high. We could hear it all the way out in the vineyard.

Johan could hear it, too. He came out of his house and yelled at us to shut down the noise. You should have seen the look on Lulu's face! She was very concerned. I motioned to Johan that we would turn it down, and Joann did. Lulu asked, "What is wrong with your neighbor? Should I go over and invite him to join us, or perhaps bring him a cookie?"

I explained the history of our relationship with Johan, and Manny shared the problem with the cows.

Though we would be head training the vines, I wanted end posts with a wire to which I could attach the irrigation pipeline up off the ground. The granite end posts were heavy, but Manny was able to position one at each end of all rows. For a frail man he was still extraordinarily strong.

Joann praised Manny, "You are amazing and very strong. It took you no time at all to dig those holes."

I told him he was a natural. Manny smiled and said, "I have not had this good of a workout since I was in football. Thank you so much for allowing me to help." Manny was joyful. Physical labor reminded him of football.

Joann and I looked at each other and smiled. It warmed our hearts. Joann told him, "We three make a good team, Manny." He smiled approvingly. He loved teams.

Joann and Lulu trimmed the plants, roots, and tops, put them in the holes, and held them while Trevor and I shoveled in the dirt. Manny placed a stake at each plant and a grow tube over the plant. Jim made sure we were all in line.

"The stake provides a support while the vine grows a strong trunk to support itself and the weight of the fruit it will bear," Jim told them, "the grow tube acts like a miniature greenhouse and protects the baby plant from nibbling animals — such as cows and rabbits."

After everything was planted, and the vineyard complete, Trevor gave me the thumbs up and said,

"Well done for a New York boy!" Joann and I invited the team for wine and cheese before they left.

Our day of planting started just as the light broke over the eastern sky. We worked hard all day until there was a brilliant sunset to the west. It was a hard but gratifying day.

As we sat on the porch admiring our work, Joann served the Messina Hof Sagrantino as a salute to the vines planted and I shared with them how much we appreciated their help. We shared with them all we had seen in Portugal and how looking out over the vineyard and granite posts, made us feel like we were part of that old world craft. I raised my glass for a toast and the others did as well.

Lulu helped Joann clean up. They talked about their lives and Joann's time in California. Lulu seemed surprised at the things they had in common and at our tolerance of such an "adversarial neighbor." "What do you plan to do about him?" she asked.

Joann smiled and answered, "I have been praying about it. You know they say the people who are the hardest to love are those that need it the most."

The next morning, one of Johan's cows was in the vineyard. I ran through the vineyard yelling and waving my hat at it. It jumped and ran back into Johan's yard. After that Johan's cows lined up at the fence with their heads through the sagging barbed wire chewing my grass and watching our progress. Johan sat in a rocking chair on his back porch, drinking a beer and glaring at us.

Chapter 15

The next glorious morning as the sun crept up above my newly planted vineyard, I saw unexpected and uninvited guests in the vineyard – Johan's cows.

At first a few of the cows made their way into the vineyard. Then, since Johan had nothing to say, other cows made their way through the fence and into the vineyard. I looked over to Johan to see if he was going to do something. Instead, he looked straight at me and continued enjoying his morning beer.

The cows enjoyed the lush green grass surrounding the vineyard. Their curious eyes scanned the area to see what was available to munch on. They seemed to enjoy exploring a new pasture with fresh grass. They reveled in their newfound freedom of my pasture and new vineyard. The cows seemed to enjoy rubbing their backs on the newly driven granite posts. I had had enough. I got on my tractor and went to see Johan.

I drove up to his fence to say hello. Just as I stepped off of the tractor, Johan went back into his house. It was obvious Johan was not interested in being a friendly neighbor.

Mary and Manny were working in their garden, so I drove to their fence line. I noticed that their lettuce had no leaves and asked them how their garden was. Manny angrily responded, "Johan's cows are visiting us daily. I hope they do not hurt the vineyard."

I asked if they had called Sheriff Bartow. Mary sighed, "We are afraid. Our dog Sonny is sick. He is unable to keep food down. Someone fed him grapes and raisins. He has had diarrhea for a week. We have never fed him grapes!

"He passed many of the grapes whole. It was obvious that they were the ones featured at the local grocery store – they were so big! They are obviously the table grapes from Greece that were promoted in the United States - Muscat of Alexandre, which the grocer says are not grown in Texas Hill Country!

"I think Johan fed Sonny the grapes as a warning message to us that calling the sheriff about his cows would lead to problems."

Mary made sure Sonny never wandered off their property again. I told Joann about the suspected poisoning by Johan because we, too, have a dog. He is a German Shepard named Prince. Prince loved chasing Johan's cows off our property and chased the cows once too many times. Johan shot Prince with a BB gun. He came running home howling.

Joann begged, "Please offer to pay for the whole new fence. Good fences make good neighbors. I don't want to lose Prince."

I offered to pay for the whole fence between our properties. I thought Johan would say no but wanted to give it one last try. Surprisingly, Johan stared at me for a few minutes. It was an awkward silence.

He finally said, "I will pay for half of the fence as soon as I can come up with the money." Then he reached out his hand and we shook on splitting the cost of the fence. It was not a friendly, welcoming handshake, but a strong, controlling handshake that was more like "let's build the fence and keep away from my cows." I think I embarrassed him when I offered to pay for all of it.

Chapter 16

Joann told me, "The agreement is a case for celebration and thanksgiving!"

She always looks for God's help in any matter and when there is an unexpected resolution, she says "Praise!" I love her.

"Johnny, we should have a party," she said. "We have so much to celebrate! The vineyard is done. We have new friends here in the Hill Country. And Johan is helping with the fence!"

I agreed and we set a date to have a family-style meal one evening in the vineyard. Joann sent out invitations to all those who had helped us settled in Fredericksburg and to all our neighbors. I hung strings of Edison lights from poles in the vineyard and moved in long, harvest-style tables in between the rows and under the lights.

"Everyone invited RSVP'd 'yes!'" she reported. "I have prepared a special menu for the evening. It is easy to prepare, and Mary said that she would help me."
I loved seeing her enthusiasm. Joann loved to entertain and loved cooking. She was in her element.

I reached out to Jim Kamas and Trevor Talan to come because they had been so supportive. Trevor asked if he could bring Lulu. I said, of course! Julio and Maria Vadus, our Portuguese friends asked if they could bring a friend. We said yes, of course. The list was growing.

The night of the event Jim and his wife, Trevor and his girlfriend Lulu, our Portuguese friends Julio and Maria Vadus and their family, Mary and Manny, Ivan and his family, and Ned from HEB arrived. As a surprise, Julio and Maria brought Count Joseph from Vinho Verde! He was visiting from Portugal and wanted to surprise us. What a pleasant reunion.

The evening was magical. The one empty chair that had been planned for Johan, who did not show up, was filled by our friend from Portugal. All things do work together for good.

Johan's back porch light was on, but he was not in his rocking chair. Ivan apologized for his dad, but I told him we were making progress and if his dad did come, we would add a chair.

Joann and Mary outdid themselves. The tables were dressed in grapevine branches, real grapes, and wine glass candles. Cork chargers, leaf lined pottery plates, and wooden handled silverware made the perfect setting. The menu incorporated Rieslings in honor of the German and Swiss friends, Sagrantino in honor of our future, and Port in honor of our Portuguese friends.

The evening started with a sparkling Riesling served with grilled peaches stuffed with honey yogurt. The next course featured fire pit roasted ribeye steaks with the Messina Hof Sagrantino that Ned had recommended, and a flight of different ports with chocolate truffles for dessert.

Count Joseph led each course with a toast. I noticed that Ivan's daughter was eyeing my guitar on the porch. I asked her, "Do you play?"

She responded, "I am learning." "Would you play for us?" I encouraged.

She nodded and went to get the guitar. She sat near the table and played for us. Soon we were all singing along. Sonny and Prince seemed to jump and dance to the music, too.

Once I looked up and saw Johan sitting on his porch, watching us. Ivan noticed too. He got up and quietly took a plate of food and some wine across the pasture to his dad. They sat together while Johan ate. There did not appear to be much conversation but there was a spirit of peace, calm, and love in their body language.

Ivan returned to the party elated, "We talked about dad's farm. He has many great memories there. He lamented that Fredericksburg is changing rapidly. Peach orchards have been pulled out and vineyards are being planted. Almost all the dairies are gone.

"I told dad that it was good that he could see these changes and that he could benefit from them. It is wonderful to cherish the past, but necessary to accept the future. He is getting old, and caring for his cows is becoming more of a burden. I told dad that I had lined up a buyer for his cows and that he would get top dollar for them."

Everyone stopped and listened. We could hear a pin drop.

"In addition, I surprised him with the fact that I was building a guest house behind my house where Johan can live and be closer to me and the family. We can take care of him."

Joann asked, "How did Johan respond to that?"

Ivan replied, "He was visibly shaken, but in a good way. He wanted to know who was buying the cows and seemed relieved that it was a friend who loved the cows as much as Johan did.

"The friend is twenty years younger and lives only five miles from my house. Dad can periodically visit the cows. He seemed resolved that this was best for him. I feel so much better."

Joann later said, "That moment between Ivan and Johan was the whole purpose of the evening. God was present there."

The next day, Ned at HEB called to offer me four tickets to this weekend's annual Fredericksburg Food and Wine Festival. I thanked Ned, jumped in my truck, and rushed to HEB to get the tickets. I called Joann on the way to share the good news. She was excited. I then called and invited Mary and Manny to join Joann and me.

Mary was quick to share the history behind the festival, "Are you familiar with Bell Mountain Vineyard? In the late 1980's Bob Oberhellmann, the owner of Bell Mountain Winery, approached the city of Fredericksburg suggesting that Fredericksburg host a Texas Wine only Wine Festival at the Fredericksburg Marketplatz.

"Bell Mountain Winery was the only winery in Gillespie County. Fortunately, the city saw the festival as a way to raise funds for the development of the downtown market square.

"The festival was to promote Texas wine, Texas food, Texas crafts and Texas music. Our Fredericksburg Convention and Visitors Bureau invited all of the well-respected Texas wineries to show their wine. Hundreds of people attended the 1991 festival. Today, more than thirty-five Texas wineries participate, and the festival is one of the finest wine festivals in the USA. Fredericksburg is second only to Napa Valley for wine tourism. It will be so much fun!"

I offered to pick them up at their home so we could drive together. They were appreciative.

Chapter 17

We knew Mary would need help with Manny down the road with his care. This festival would be a wonderful opportunity to meet the Hill Country wineries and to spend more time with our neighbors. Besides, Manny was so proud of his participation in the Boone Vineyard. He went out every day to check the baby vines to see how they were growing.

One morning when he went out, Johan's cows were in our vineyard despite the new fence. The baby vines were just peeking above the grow tubes. The tender leaves were too tempting for the cows. They just had to taste this new offering across the fence. I jumped in the four-wheeler and started driving through the vineyard honking the horn trying to herd the cows back across the fence.

Manny ran out with BB gun shooting over the heads of the cows to scare them away. The gun made a loud popping sound. The cows ignored the shot. Manny shot again, and he hit a big brown cow in the hind quarter. The cow jumped. Manny ran after the cow and shot his BB gun again, hitting the second brown cow in the hind quarter. That cow also jumped.

Manny proceeded to shoot thirty cows in the hind quarter and then ran after all of them until they were back on Johan's side of the fence. When Manny told me what he did, I asked if Johan was sitting on the porch. Manny said he was not there. I told Manny not to do that again. Manny thought that because it was only a BB gun, the cows would hardly realize that they had been shot. He did not stop until every cow was back on Johan's land. Johan, who had now arrived outside, just sat there, and watched.

Manny was furious. He asked, "What can we do to protect the grapes from these cows?"

I told him we might need to cover the plants with netting, but that we would get more insight from some growers at the festival.

As I drove to get the tickets, I passed the Hill Country Gun Shop where I noticed Johan's pickup truck parked outside and made a mental note to share the info with the Effors and with Joann.

Ned was at the HEB and greeted me with tickets in hand. I told him thank you and gave him an update on the vineyard. He was so encouraging, "That is great, Johnny, I cannot wait to taste the wine from your grapes. Let me know when you have your first harvest, and I will be there."

Mary, Manny, Joann, and I drove together to the festival. Every parking space was filled. Downtown was swarming with people.

Mary and Manny had seen this before, "People from all over Texas and other states come to this festival. The merchants love it because it kicks off the holiday season when they make most of their money.

"Drive beyond the Marketplatz in the center of town, John, and park near the Fredericksburg Farmers' Market. From there we can enter the festival but also be near enough to walk to the Pioneer Museum, which is in downtown Fredericksburg."

Joann suggested, "Why don't we go to the Pioneer Museum first?" Everyone agreed.

At the museum, we started our tour with a video of the area's history. Our guide shared, "In the mid-1840's, Germans started moving into the Hill Country by way of New Orleans and Galveston, Texas. The Pioneer Museum tells the story of those original settlers.

"There are ten original buildings from the era. In 1955, the historical society bought the historic Kammlah house store and property. Joe Kammlah, an ancestor of the family, returned home to Fredericksburg to develop our Convention and Visitors Bureau as the editor of the Fredericksburg newspaper. He had been the editor of the Bryan newspaper. His family originated in Fredericksburg.

"There are more than 300,000 artifacts housed in the Pioneer Museum. The People's Church, a replica of the first public building in Fredericksburg, is found here. The church served as a fort, a town hall, school, and church. The original church was demolished in 1896."

We wandered through the buildings. Joann and Mary were particularly interested in the completely furnished Kammlah house and kitchen. Manny and I were amazed at the smoke house construction. I wondered if they had ever made those half-smokes there. We had a wonderful time touring the museum and then walked down to the wine festival.

Chapter 18

At the festival, we tasted many great wines. I was particularly interested in the Messina Hof tasting table. They were serving the Messina Hof Sagrantino Reserva. I told the server that Joann and I had moved from New York and that we were putting in five acres of Sagrantino.

She eagerly told us, "One of the founders, Paul Vincent, was from New York in the Bronx. He and his wife, Merrill, co-founded Messina Hof Winery. It is now owned by their next generation. Their son is the winemaker. Paul and Merrill were the ones who brought Sagrantino to Texas.

"Merrill's great-grandfather, Martin Kuno Sachs, was from Hof, Germany. He was a resourceful German immigrant who worked in this area as a stone mason building the courthouses on the Hill Country town squares like Fredericksburg, Bandera, Blanco, Llano, and Lampasas. He also received a US Patent on the automated brick making machine.

"He was born in Hof, Bavaria and always considered himself a Prussian. He arrived in Fredericksburg in the late 1800's. Imagine how Merrill Bonarrigo's great-grandfather helped to settle Fredericksburg and Messina Hof helped to pioneer winemaking in Fredericksburg and Texas. Pioneering is in the gene pool!

"You should check with Messina Hof to see if they would be interested in contracting your grapes. You know, Messina Hof is the largest producer of Sagrantino in the United States and the first to introduce the grape to Texas."

She poured each of us a taste. It was fun tasting the Sagrantino in a festival environment compared to many other wines. Joann and I love big, bold reds. This wine was the biggest and boldest I had tasted.

Joann smiled, "It is yummy!" That is her way of saying it is delicious and well balanced. Hitting a "yummy" on her scale is not easy.

I was elated. It would be an honor to have our grapes in this wine. I would love to be part of the Messina Hof grower family!

Manny asked for another glass. I was surprised when he reached over and tipped the bottle a little more to get a bigger pour. That was presumptuous, I thought.

Joann and I looked at each other. We did not even know if Manny liked wine.

Manny moved ahead of us. He gulped his wine and moved to the next table. As he drank, he became overly aggressive, cutting in line and pushing his way to the tables. At one table, he pushed a man who pushed back. Suddenly, Manny recognized the man as Johnny P. He became even more angry. They began to throw punches. A security guard broke up the fight and escorted Johnny P to the first aid tent and looked to Mary to take care of Manny. The guard recognized Manny and had a protective heart for him.

Mary suggested, "Manny, let's go sit down and enjoy the music." He ignored her and continued to move through the crowd like in his football days.

Finally, we gathered around him and led him to the food tent, where we found German sausage on a stick. Joann and I stayed with them until I knew Manny was under control. Then, we left them there to eat while Joann and I went to taste more wines and meet more Hill Country vintners.

At one table, there was a large football player looking at a guy pouring wine. He wore a big cowboy hat and had a smile as big as he was. He introduced himself as Tommy Jest and his wife Mary. I recognized him immediately. He was one of my heroes when he played in the National Football League.

I was so impressed that a National Football League player was growing grapes in Texas. Maybe it was not such a stretch for a New Yorker to grow Sagrantino along the Pedernales River.

Two other couples were standing there. Tommy introduced us, "These fine folks write about wine and our Texas wine industry. You should get to know them. This is Dillard and Reno Costello and Flip and Flow Adams. They have been promoting Texas wines for years."

We talked about some of their experiences in the Hill Country. They asked if we had been to Luckenbach.

Joann said, "We have heard of it. It is on our bucket list, but we have not been." They encouraged us to go.

After we finished tasting, we gathered Mary and Manny and walked back to our car. We talked about all that we had learned at the museum and at the festival.

I wondered what Merrill's great-grandfather must have experienced as an immigrant working here. He was a pioneer. Joann and I felt like pioneers.

Chapter 19

From the wine festival in the market square, we got into the car and drove to Luckenbach. Along the way, we passed the Texas Tech University Hill Country Campus, the Alstadt Brewery, many beautiful vineyards, and peach orchards.

In Luckenbach, we listened to great Texas music. Joann likes to explore. She was fascinated by the tiny post office there, "Look at this little post office. It is a tiny store. Look at the saloon. Can you imagine what stories these walls could tell?"

Mary shared, "One of the first settlers in the 1800's in our area was Jacob Luckenbach. He came from German nobility to find riches in Texas. Can you imagine what a surprise he and his family encountered in this undeveloped wild west?" Everyone laughed.

Encouraged by everyone's enjoyment she added, "Well, he had those good German stubbornness, determinedness, and resourcefulness traits. With other Germans in the area, he started the town as a trading post that catered to all sorts of needs."

Joann looked at me and said, "Close your eyes and envision Jacob Luckenbach coming upon this land in the mid-1800's. There was nothing here. Now, fast forward to us listening to Waylon and Willie at their July 4th concerts in this same place!"

Mary added, "Did you know that Luckenbach was sold – lock, stock, and barrel? The family that owned the town in the 70's sold it to a group of larger-than-life Texans. What do larger-than-life Texans do? They make anything they touch colorful and creative.

"They turned Luckenbach into a sort of Western themed Renfest busy with singing, dancing, and partying. It always gives a feeling of belonging, like the town itself only exists in the hearts of those present."

History was everywhere. I sensed that we were about to make our own history. As we sat and listened to the music, we talked about our backgrounds and what brought us to this common place. It has always interested me how the Lord brings different people into our lives for even just a small part of our journeys here on earth. I wondered what our journey with the Effors would be.

The subject changed to our common neighbor Johan and his cows. I shared with them that I had seen Johan's truck at the gun shop.

Mary looked worried and asked, "How are we going to get Johan's cows off the property?"

Manny growled, "He just needs to be responsible for his cows. Or he could pay us for damages."

Joann calmly interceded, "That will only make things worse. Why don't we invite his son Ivan over for lunch?"

Mary volunteered, "I will call him."

We all met for lunch at the Fredericksburg Brewing Company. It is one of our favorite spots and I love their Porter beer.

Ivan was very sympathetic, but he said, "Johan is very stubborn. I will try to talk with him for you, but I can almost guarantee that he will not listen to me. Besides, he told me you had gone in together to put up a new fence. If he did not think it would help, why would he pay for half of it?"

I told Ivan the cows walked right through the new fence.

"I contacted several fence builders to see if there was more we could do to the fence to keep out the cows. The fence builders recommended we electrify the new fence."

Ivan said he was concerned that the electric fence would hurt Johan's beloved cows. Ivan promised to talk with his dad the next day. Mary and Manny thanked Ivan and headed home.

Joann suggested, "Ivan, let's stop at the Old German Bakery and get some pastries for your dad. We will pay for the pastries, and you can take them with you. What does your dad like?"

Ivan responded, "He loves their Apples in Dressing Gowns. That might soften Johan's heart about the idea of selling the cows or at least allowing the addition of an electric fence. I have been after him so long to get rid of them so that he could spend more time being a grandfather to my children."

Not only did we walk out of the bakery with the pastries but the recipe, too! Joann was ecstatic.

Apples in Dressing Gowns

Filling:

    2 apples, peeled and cored
    1 cup raisins, soaked overnight in enough Messina Hof Port
    to cover raisins.
    1 teaspoon cinnamon
    ¼ teaspoon cloves
    ¼ teaspoon nutmeg
    Pinch of ginger
    1 tablespoon butter
    ½ cup Messina Hof Angel Riesling
    ½ cup water
    1 cup sugar
    1 tablespoon lemon juice

Pastry:

    1 egg
    ½ teaspoon vanilla
    3 tablespoons butter, room temperature
    ½ cup sifted flour
    Pinch of salt

1. Sauté two apples in butter turning on all sides of the apple
    for 3 to 5 minutes. Set aside saucepan with apples in it. Boil
    the rest of the filling ingredients, except raisins in port wine,
    for 5 minutes. Pour over apples and cook uncovered until
    apples are tender, and liquid has become syrupy.

2. Prepare pastry. Beat egg with vanilla and 1 ½ tablespoons
    butter until creamy. Gradually add flour and salt. Knead 15
    minutes or until you can stretch the dough to as close to
    paper thin as you can get without breaking. Roll into a ball
    and cut into two pieces.

3. Roll dough into a circle on flour dusted pastry board. The
    dough circle should be large enough to envelope one of the
    apples.

4. Drain raisins and set aside the pot for later use.

5. Place apple in center of dough circle. Fill cored hollow with raisins. Drizzle with syrup to fill the rest of core and lightly coat apple. Sprinkle with a pinch of cinnamon and pinch of sugar. Bring dough up around apple and seal edges to make a ball.

6. Complete second apple in the same way. Put both in a lightly greased pan. Brush each with remaining butter. Bake at 400 degrees F until pastry is golden, about 15-20 minutes or until golden brown.

7. Simmer port with remaining raisins until it reaches syrup consistency. Serve Apples in Dressing Gowns warm from the oven, drizzled with remaining raisins and syrup. Top with whipped cream.

Chapter 20

"Good morning!" I was barely awake. "Good morning, sweetheart," sang Joann. She had such a soft, melodic voice.

"Guess what I have for you this morning," she teased. "Apples in Dressing Gowns with espresso!"

She served me breakfast in bed. It had been a long time since she surprised me with that morning greeting. Before we moved to Texas, we took turns on the weekend serving the other breakfast in bed.

My specialty was making sunny side eggs with happy faces. I would fry the eggs, then put pesto for eyebrows and ketchup for lips. Oregano made great hair. Joann was so sweet and made me feel that she liked it.

She liked my espresso because I brewed it strong and added a small amount of chocolate liquor and topped it with whipped cream. She said it was a culinary masterpiece. I loved seeing the whip cream stick to her nose as she sipped her espresso.

"This is delicious," exclaimed Joann, "it is the best espresso ever."

As we read our newspaper, we talked about the upcoming music in Luckenbach and local wine tastings."

I was sipping my coffee when I got a frantic call from Ivan.

He sobbed, "As I drove to dad's house this morning to take him the Apples in Dressing Gowns, there was an unusual stillness. Normally the cows would line up to greet me with mooing sounds. Instead, there were no cows in sight and there was silence.

"I walked through the front door and called to dad, but there was no answer. I looked through the back door to the porch and saw his silhouette in the morning sun. He was sitting in his usual rocking chair. I called his name again as I approached but there was no answer and no movement. My heart froze.

"As I approached, I saw blood all over the back porch! Dad was slumped over in the chair, his .357 gun in his hand and a pool of blood surrounding him. He was shot in the head!"

Ivan began to cry as he whispered, "He is dead. There is no note. What happened? Did you hear anything? What should I do?"

I told him, "We heard nothing, Ivan. We are so sorry for your loss. What a shock! All has been quiet since we returned home the night before. You should call the sheriff. Joann and I will be right over."

I immediately called Trevor and Jim. Jim did not answer, so I left a message.

Trevor answered and told me to wait for him. "I will be right there," he said.

On the way, Joann and I talked about what might have happened. We did not know if Johan had taken his own life, or if there was there something much more sinister at play.

I felt sorry for Ivan and knew his heart was broken. I told Joann, "Johan was a stern man, but a loving father, and now he is gone before the Lord had the chance to soften his heart so he could be an important part of Ivan's children's lives."

Joann caressed my hand, "The Lord's timing is perfect. His ways are a mystery to us but can bring revelation and change to our lives – even Johan's life." Ivan was on the phone with Sheriff Bartow when we arrived.

Ivan was explaining, "Dad did not answer. I came as soon as I could. The cows were acting strangely as though everything had changed. The house was dark and quiet as I entered. I called his name, but he did not answer. As I approached the back door, I saw his silhouette slumped in his favorite rocking chair. There was no movement. There was no response."

Sheriff Bartow instructed him, "Please leave everything as it is, do not disturb the scene, and wait for me there. I am on the way."

Ivan seemed very frazzled. On the way to be with him, we had seen Mary and Manny working in their gardens. They waved. I did not have the heart to tell them what had happened, and I wanted to get to Ivan as soon as I could.

Right after we arrived, Trevor showed up. He introduced himself to Sheriff Bartow, who had arrived a few minutes earlier. Trevor asked me if there was any damage to the vineyard.

I shrugged and said that I had not even looked. "So many other things have been happening."

Trevor excused himself and went out the back door.

Chapter 21

Sheriff Bartow arrived on the scene with Dr. Hemlow, the county coroner. Dr. Hemlow was a retired pathologist from Munich, Germany. He had family in Fredericksburg, so he and his wife, Nurse Betty Hemlow, moved into the community three years ago. Before Dr. Hemlow arrived, coroners would come from Austin.

As Sheriff Bartow examined the scene, he noticed, "Johan was shot in the left temple area. Johan was right-handed." He paused and looked at Ivan, "If he were to shoot himself, he would have shot himself in the right temple."

Dr. Hemlow placed the time of the death at two am and then added, "If Johan were going to kill himself, why would he wait until 2 am? Plus, there are only two cans of beer here, and the second can is half full. Were there two people present?"

Both men agreed that Johan was killed with his own weapon by someone else. Suddenly, what appeared to be a suicide became a murder.

"Who could have been the second person?" I asked Dr. Hemlow.

"Time will tell. Let's look at the evidence," he said.

Trevor walked in from the vineyard, approached Sheriff Bartow, and shared, "Someone has cut the wires on the trellis in the vineyard. This takes time and a plan."

The Sheriff asked who would have wanted to cut the trellis wires. I told him, "Johan did not want the vineyards here. I think he still felt it was his land. He just stared at us from his back porch."

The Sheriff thanked me and walked away. Trevor suggested that the wire cutting was an act of anger or hatred.

Johan's body was taken by Dr. Hemlow, the coroner, to his lab for closer inspection. Sheriff Bartow sealed the scene and took many pictures of the porch. He then turned to the neighbors.

Sheriff Bartow asked me to bring Joann to his office. That night there was a raging thunderstorm. Rain beat down on our roof. I had difficulty staying asleep. I was not accustomed to so much thunder. In New York we rarely had such thunderous storms.

The next morning as we drove to Sheriff Bartow's office, we saw many tree limbs that had fallen in the gusty winds of the night. He greeted us at the door. I could tell Sheriff Bartow was not accustomed to conducting murder investigations. He was sweating profusely, asked us to sit down, and began asking questions.

"Where were you and Joann last night?" he asked.

"We were in Luckenbach listening to music with our neighbors, Mary and Manny Effors."

Sheriff continued, "When was the last time you saw Johan?"

I shared that I saw Johan's truck at the Hill Country Gun Shop yesterday afternoon.

"Has there been any unusual activity on your or Johan's property that you are aware of?"

"No," I answered, "but I did approach Johan about the fence, and his son Ivan tried to convince Johan to sell his cows. Johan just responded, 'no need'."

Joann chirped, "We even bought Apples in Dressing Gowns for Ivan to give to Johan."

Sheriff Bartow dismissed us and thanked us for our time.

When we got home, Joann walked out to the porch edge and called for Prince to come. He did not come. She called again. Prince did not come. Joann looked worried and then looked at me as though I would have an answer.

Chapter 22

I walked the property, shouting over and over, *'Here Prince, come to Papa!'* Tears welled up in my eyes when I saw a dog hanging from a vineyard post at the far end of the property. As I got closer, I could see it was our beloved Prince. He had been shot and strung up on the post. I also noticed that the vineyard wires were cut.

I called Sheriff Bartow to tell him what happened to our dog. I asked him what the gun shop owner said about Johan's gun.

He said the owner told him, "Johan bought a .357 caliber, and he told me that he would be doing some hunting. Johan also said he needed the gun for protection."

Sheriff Bartow brought Dr. Hemlow with him to our vineyard. They gently removed Prince from the vineyard post and took him back to Dr. Hemlow's office. He told me that he would discover the caliber of the weapon that killed Prince.

Joann was in disbelief, "How could this happen? Who would do such a thing?" She called Mary to warn her for Sonny's safety.

Mary answered, "Hi Joann, we had so much fun with you at Luckenbach the other night. Thank you for the invitation."

"Our pleasure, Mary, it was a joy to get to spend more time with you. But today I have sad news and a warning for you."

Mary said, "What is it, Joann? A warning about what?"

Joann told her about Johan's death, which appeared to be a murder, and the story about Prince. I overheard her say, "Please protect Sonny. I do not know who did this, but they might try to come again."

Sheriff Bartow left us to go to the Hill Country Gun Shop.

Mary sighed, "If Johan were murdered, who could have done it? Whoever did it is still out there."

She thanked Joann for calling and said, "I am so sorry for your loss, Joann, you know there are a lot of hunters in town. Sheriff Bartow is a good man. He will help us. He knows Manny's situation and is kind to talk football with him whenever he sees him. I will wait for his call."

Sheriff Bartow showed up at their door and Mary answered. She told him, "We are so sorry to hear about Johan. What a sad day!"

He asked where they had been. She explained that they had gone to Luckenbach with the Boone's. "We came home and went to bed," she said, "There must have been fireworks during the night, but it was brief. It woke me up. Manny slept through them. He gets up frequently during the night but slept through that.

"He had such a full day with lots of wine, so he was very tired. The lighting storm was fierce. The wind must have been gusting more than forty miles per hour. Then, as fast as the lightning came and the wind blew, it all stopped. The storm only lasted ten minutes."

Sheriff Bartow asked, "What about your dog Sonny? I know he means the world to Manny and would hate for anything to happen to him. Where is he?"

Mary looked at Manny and then at Sheriff Bartow, "I guess we have not seen him today. We have been busy in the garden."

Sheriff Bartow noticed that Manny's face seemed to cloud up just for a second. He asked, "Do you mind if I walk the property? I want to make sure you are secure."

Mary said it was fine, "I am sure everything is ok, but thank you for checking."

As he walked, Sheriff Bartow received a phone call from Dr. Hemlow confirming there were no powder burns on Johan's head nor powder residue on his hands.

The doctor said, "I am 99% sure Johan was killed. We are looking at murder."

Sheriff Bartow walked the Effor's property with a new purpose. I saw him as he crossed our property to Johan's. He walked the old 'fought-over' fence line between our property and Johan's property. In the distance I could see him stop, bend down, and look to the north.

Trevor joined us at my request. He ran out to us to see what was going on. When Sheriff Bartow had walked the fence line, he saw a trail of blood coming from Johan's property toward the Pedernales River.

Trevor grabbed a shovel from his truck and went toward the river. We followed him. There, we found large boot-prints coming from the river to Johan's house. By the river, Sheriff Bartow found a clearing where brush had been removed. In that space there was a mound of newly dug dirt.

He paused as though to say a prayer about what he was about to find. He looked at us and said, "I think we may find Sonny here."

I watched as Trevor gently dug away the dirt from the mound. As suspected, Sonny was there in the grave. My heart tightened.

Trevor shook his head and said, "Whoever did this was angry. Whoever cut all your trellis wires was angry about something, too. Be careful."

"I am going to talk with Mary and Manny," Sheriff Bartow said calmly, "you should go home. It is not safe to be out here all alone."
Trevor insisted, "I will go with you."

I walked back toward home and watched Sheriff Bartow and Trevor slowly stroll toward the Effor's home.

Chapter 23

Along the way, Trevor shared with Sheriff Bartow that the wire that I had used on the trellis system was a much heavier duty wire than normal. "It would have taken a heavy-duty wire cutter and a lot of labor to cut all those wires. Who would have had the time, the tools, and the desire to do it?"

Sheriff Bartow looked at Trevor and said, "Who would have been invested enough in the trellis system to be offended by its destruction?"

Trevor nodded and responded, "Installing that trellis system was one of the most important jobs that Manny has done. He took great pride in it."

Sheriff Bartow rang the doorbell. Mary opened the door and warmly invited him to join them. "Manny is watching his Most Valuable Player Superbowl tapes," she said. "Can I get you something to drink?"

"No thank you, Mary, I just need to talk with Manny."

She showed him the way. He walked in with his hat in his hand. After a brief pause, staring at Manny and then at the Superbowl videos, he said, "Hi, Manny, where is Sonny?"

Manny looked at him and Mary and began to cry. "He is in heaven," he said.

"Where is Johan, Manny?" asked Sheriff Bartow.

Manny looked at him with the fierceness of a Superbowl Most Valuable Player. "Johan should be in hell," he shouted, "I think he killed Sonny."

Mary could not believe what she was hearing. "No," she yelled as she looked from Manny to Sheriff Bartow, "this cannot be right. Manny does not know what he is saying. "

Trevor suggested that everyone should sit down to talk. He said to Manny, "You did a great job with the vineyard and the trellis system. You must feel very proud. John and Joann so appreciate all that you did."

Manny responded, "It was the first time in a long time that I felt like I was part of a team. They truly appreciated me. I took a great deal of pride in that vineyard.

"When we got home from the wonderful time at Luckenbach and I saw the wires in the vineyard cut, I was so angry."

Manny was sitting in his chair covered with a quilt and with a knit cap pulled down over his ears. It was not even that cold. He looked at Mary with downcast eyes as though he had failed. "I tried to protect Sonny after I saw Prince strung on the end post. Prince died. I know Johan killed both dogs."

Sheriff Bartow asked Manny, "How do you know Johan killed the dogs?"

Manny slowly shared that when they arrived home from Luckenbach, he went to sit in the backyard garden in the dark by the firepit.

"I had too much to drink and needed to clear my head," he said. "The air was cool, and the fire was warm. In the dark, I saw the silhouette of a man that looked like Johan dragging an animal across the pasture to the end of the property line. He appeared to be deliberately walking through the vineyard rows cutting the wires as he went. Then he disappeared from my view behind the trees.

After about fifteen minutes, the same silhouette trudged through the pasture to Johan's house and went inside. I knew it must have been him."

Sheriff Bartow completed Manny's thought for him, "So you assumed Johan had disposed of an animal, but you did not know what it was?"

Manny nodded yes.

Sheriff Bartow asked, "Manny, have you seen anyone else out on this property?

He answered, "We had a nice party the other night. Several people were in the vineyard. A group of strangers came from town. Someone told me they were media. They wanted to see the vineyard."

Sheriff Bartow became suspicious, "Manny, I feel like you are not telling me everything. I find it hard to believe that you watched someone walk from Johan's house to the river and back and you did nothing."

Manny looked like a child caught in a lie. He said, "I walked toward the river to see what was there. It was then that I saw Prince hanging from the vineyard end post. It was so sad. I knew that Johnny and Joann would be so hurt." He looked at the sheriff and said, "They are my friends. They are like family and so was Prince.

"After I saw Prince, I called for Sonny. Sonny did not come. Something in my heart told me that the person who killed Prince had also harmed Sonny."

Manny stared across the room and continued, "Anger filled me. I could not take it anymore. Hatred overcame me. I ran to Johan's house. As I got closer, I could see Johan sitting on his porch rocking in his chair as though nothing had happened. I saw his gun on the porch at his feet and told him that I saw Prince hanging. And I told him that I saw him walking back to his house. 'Why would you kill Prince?' I asked.

He looked at me and said, "The dogs are annoying my cows." He said it so calmly with no remorse.

I said, "'dogs'? What dogs?" He was obviously talking about more than Prince, and I suddenly realized that he had also killed Sonny.

"I went into a rage and grabbed Johan by the collar, demanding to know where he put Sonny. He fought back, grabbed his gun, and tried to shoot me. He got off a shot that grazed my left ear and the second shot got me in the left thigh just above my knee."

The quilt covering and knit cap suddenly made sense. Manny had given himself first aid and was hiding the wounds.

He lamented, "I grabbed the gun from Johan, but he jumped on me, and we fell to the ground. On impact, the gun went off, striking Johan in the head. He went lifeless. There was no pulse. I knew that Johan was dead.

"I put him back in his chair, wiped the gun and put it in his hand. It took me a while to limp home. My left leg was wounded – the same knee that ended my career and is already in bad shape. The bullet made it worse.

"Mary was asleep. Quietly, I took off my blood-soaked clothes, burned them in the garden fire pit, cleaned my wounds, and slept in my chair."

He looked at Mary. "I had to protect us, Mary," he said. "Johan was killing our garden and destroying the vineyard that I cared so much about. He killed our Sonny, and he did not care."

Sheriff Bartow shared with Mary and Manny where he had found Sonny. He allowed them time to hug and cry. Then he took Manny into custody. Manny asked if he could wear his Cowboy jersey. Mary followed him, wailing with a broken heart.

Chapter 24

Manny was quite the celebrity when he was booked in the jail. The newspapers ran his photo and story. The whole town rallied around him. Many of his teammates came to town to support him at the trial. I realized what a loyal and tight family the National Football League players were.

Everyone makes mistakes. Everyone has the capacity to break when pushed beyond what they are able. I realized for myself that my faith was what helped me to remain balanced and calm under duress. It is not my own power that sustains me but a greater power that helps me.

The District Attorney charged Manny with involuntary manslaughter, claiming that the killing occurred in the heat of passion as a result of provocation. Manny was also charged with tampering with the evidence because he staged the scene to look like a suicide.

Manny and Mary hired Mr. Spencer West to represent Manny at trial. Mr. West had attended Baylor Law School and was the most famous attorney in Gillespie County. At Mr. West's advice, Manny pled not guilty.

He claimed it was self-defense. The trial was the biggest news in Fredericksburg.

The first witness for the prosecution was the coroner. The coroner said the wound that killed Johan came from his own gun. The bullet penetrated Johans' head in the left temporal area. He reported, "Johan died immediately from the gunshot wound. There was no residual powder residue found on Johan's left hand. There were bruises on Johan's arms and trunk, and his clothing was torn signifying that there had been a struggle before he was shot. It looked as though Johan died the evening before his body was discovered."

The defense had no questions.

The second witness was Sheriff Bartow. He said, "When I arrived on the scene, Johan was sitting in his rocking chair. It was obvious he was shot in the left temporal region. Johan was holding his gun in his left hand. I knew Johan was right-handed.

"There were large boot footprints in the dirt off of the porch and there were scuff marks on the porch that looked like there was a fight.

"Johan's shirt and pants were ripped. He looked like he had been in quite a fight, yet he was positioned in his rocking chair with the gun placed in his left hand."

The sheriff then testified that he knew there was bad blood between Johan and Manny. "Johan filed a complaint about both dogs harassing his cows. Manny filed a complaint about Johan threatening to damage the vineyard."

The District Attorney said that he had no more questions for the sheriff.

Manny's attorney asked the sheriff in cross-examination, "In your opinion was Johan a disturbed person subject to anger and violence.

 Sheriff Bartow answered, "Yes."

Mr. West said he had no more questions.
The prosecution called Ivan to the stand.

"What was Johan's state of mind regarding his neighbors prior to his death?"

Ivan testified, "Johan appeared to have finally made peace with his neighbors. He had decided to sell the property and his cows and was going to move into my guest house."

The prosecutor had no other questions for Ivan.

Mr. West cross-examined Ivan, "Are you aware that your father purchased a gun?"

"Yes, I am aware."

"Are you aware of why he bought the gun?"
Ivan responded, "When I questioned my father about it, he said it was for protection."

Mr. West asked, "Were you aware that Johan's relationship with Manny and the Boones was confrontational?"

Ivan reflected that he knew his dad was very combative. "I was conflicted. I also knew that Manny did not like Johan."

"Ivan, were you aware that Johan did not like his neighbors and disliked their dogs? Remember that you are under oath."

"I knew that Johan had been fighting with his neighbors over the shared fences and the dogs that were harassing his cows.

"I thought Johan moving into my guest house would resolve the bad blood that existed between all the parties."

The prosecution rested.

Mr. West called the gun shop owner to the stand. "What did Johan tell you about why he was getting a gun?"

The shop owner replied, "He said he was getting the gun to keep his neighbors' dogs away from his cows. Johan was very agitated when he bought the gun. He said he had lived out in the country with his cows for so many years and that his neighbors were causing him to change his life.

"He said it was forcing him to sell his land and to move in with his son."

Mr. West called Trevor Talan to the stand. "Trevor, how do you know Manny?"

"I was a consultant on Mr. Boone's vineyard project. Manny was helping the Boone's plant the vineyard."

"How was Manny's general behavior?"

"Manny appeared to be a very gentle soul. He had episodes of forgetfulness. But he was very caring about this vineyard project and really appreciated the Boone family. He enjoyed working in the garden with his wife, Mary, and in the vineyard with his neighbors, the Boone's."

In cross examination the prosecutor asked Trevor, "How did Manny feel about his neighbor, Johan?"

Trevor responded, "Manny told me that he thought Johan was a threat to the vineyard and to the dogs."

Chapter 25

Manny asked to be put on the stand. Both Mr. West and Mary told him it was a bad idea. Manny insisted. Mr. West put Manny on the stand. It was a very dangerous thing to do.

Mr. West asked, "Manny, why did you think Johan killed the dogs?"

"I knew that Johan hated the dogs, and I saw a male silhouette dragging an object through the vineyard and carrying a shovel. Then, I saw the same silhouette return to Johan's house without the object, but still carrying the shovel.

"I had to go and speak to Johan, so I went to his porch to confront him with my belief that he had killed the dogs. Johan admitted to me that he had killed the dogs and that he was glad they were gone."

"He seemed to take pleasure in what he had done. I saw that Johan had a gun next to his right hand, and I could tell he had been drinking. There was an empty bottle of bourbon sitting next to his chair."

Manny continued, "I just went over to talk to him and ask about the death of the Boone's dog, Prince.

"When I asked him about Prince, he became enraged, raised his gun, and shot me grazing my ear. He did not hesitate and shot me again. The bullet went straight through my thigh muscle.

"I jumped on Johan to try to take the gun away from him. We struggled, rolling around on the porch. The gun went off. Johan went limp. I pulled away and saw that he had been shot in the head.

"I knew I could hardly stand. My leg was bleeding badly. I put Johan back in his chair and checked for a pulse and discovered that he was dead.

"I picked up the gun and placed it in his left hand because the wound was on the left side of his head. I panicked and hobbled back to my house.

"Mary was asleep. I dressed my wounds and stopped the bleeding."

Mr. West asked, "Manny, how do you feel about Joann and Johnny?"

After a long pause Manny seemed confused and asked, "Who are they?"

Mr. West responded, "You remember Joann and Johnny, your next-door neighbors?"

Manny smiled, "Oh, you mean the Boone's, my neighbors. I loved them and their dog Prince. He got along so well with Sonny."

Mr. West had no further questions.
The prosecution asked, "Why did you kill Johan? Do you not recognize that if you had not gone there, Johan would still be alive today?"

The judge asked Manny if he needed time to compose himself. Manny replied in a broken voice, "I'm OK, judge."

The prosecutor says, "Manny, do you need me to repeat the question?"

"I thought that I could just have a conversation with Johan about the dogs. I never imagined that it could escalate to what happened."

"Manny, aren't you a lot bigger than Johan? Are we to believe that you could not disarm him?"

"He had the gun. He shot me. I was trying to get the gun away from him."

The prosecutor asked, "Manny, why when you knew that you had killed Johan would you make it look like he had killed himself?"

Manny said, "I was afraid that no one would believe the fact that I, an all-pro National Football League football player, struggled with an elderly man like Johan."

Manny began to cry. I looked around the gallery and saw the sorrow in the faces of his NFL teammates as they realized the effects of Manny's dementia.

With tears in his eyes, Manny confessed, "I never meant to hurt Johan."

The prosecution had no more questions.

The defense rested.

Chapter 26

In the prosecutors summation, he reiterated the fact that Manny provoked the death of Johan. He deliberately went to Johan's porch and confronted him. Now Johan is dead, and Manny is responsible for his death.

Manny, realizing that he had killed Johan, then manipulated the crime scene and tampered with the evidence, staging the scene to look like a suicide. This constitutes tampering with evidence and obstructing justice by attempting to mislead law enforcement by making it look self-inflicted.

Mr. West began his summation, "Manny is an All-Star NFL player who has never had any run-ins with the law. Manny has dementia. He tried to have a civil conversation with Johan. Johan shot Manny twice and he had no choice but to try to defend himself. In the ensuing struggle with Johan, the gun went off, striking and killing him. This is a clear case of self-defense. Due to Manny's dementia, he panicked and placed Johan in the chair fearing that no one would believe him. Johan is the aggressor in this case. Manny was the victim. Members of the jury, you should not find the defendant guilty of either charge. Thank you."

The judge provided instructions to the jury, and they went out to deliberate.

It was in the hands of the jury. The gallery was filled with Manny's admirers. He was their local celebrity. They loved him. After deliberating for two hours, the jury returned with a verdict of not guilty of involuntary manslaughter. The jury did find Manny guilty of tampering with the evidence but suggested leniency.

The judge sentenced Manny to probation, realizing that Manny's dementia would be limiting his life. Mary and Manny were greatly relieved and appreciative of the judges' sensitivity to Manny's condition.

He was able to continue on as normal, but as time went on, his life became very limited.

Sheriff Bartow visited Manny. They talked about Manny's days as a Cowboy until Manny could no longer recall those memories.

I remembered meeting Tommy Jest, one of his National Football League friends, and contacting him about Manny's condition. Tommy even came to visit him. He and Manny talked about the old NFL days.

We visited Manny almost daily and updated him on the vineyard. Mary ministered to her husband with her beautiful spirit of love.

Manny would come to town, visit the bakery, and tell the same stories over and over. Everyone loved Manny, so they listened as though they were hearing the story for the first time.

After a while, Manny could no longer go into town. He had difficulty walking, so his fans would drive out to his house. Manny would hold court. His spirit brightened up every time someone came to visit.

Many of his NFL friends started having symptoms of their own. The month before Manny died, a Dallas reporter came to interview Manny. He was as bright as ever. Physically, he was weak, but his spirit was strong.

Manny's condition worsened. He died peacefully with Mary and us at his side. Sheriff Bartow, Trevor, and I were Manny's pallbearers at the funeral, along with some of his teammates.

Mary sold me her land and moved to Dallas to be close to friends. Ivan continued growing his construction company. He sold Johan's cows at the auction barn and sold Johan's land to me. He thought it was the right thing to do, since the Boone Family Vineyard was growing and we needed more acreage.

Joann took enology classes at Texas Tech in Fredericksburg and became a winemaker for our new winery. I was so proud of her. She brought joy to the winery. Everyone loved coming to work. We were like a family.

I became good friends with Jim Kamas and Trevor Talan and learned so much about Hill Country grapes. We have become one of the largest vineyards in the Hill Country and are still growing!

Messina Hof Winery is our partner winery. They buy some of our grapes. Thank you to the Lord for connecting us at the Fredericksburg Food and Wine Festival. Planting Sagrantino was our best decision, and we are so proud to have our grapes in Messina Hof's Sagrantino Reserva.

Primary Fictional Characters

John and Joann Boone were born and raised in New York. John worked for a large computer company. Joann was a teacher.

Manny and Mary Effors played for the University of Miami. His father was a scout for the New York Giants and tried to protect him through his high school career. Once Manny got to Miami University, his dad could not protect him any longer. His years of play left him injured physically and mentally.

Johan Nessel is a farmer and cow herder whose family was from Switzerland. He lost his wife and young daughter and has a strained relationship with his son, **Ivan**.

Ned is a Texas Hill Country Wine Steward

Trevor Talan is a Viticulturist working for Texas A&M University and an investigator. He travels the state. His girlfriend is **Lulu**

Sheriff Bartow

Dennis Kusy

About the Authors

Paul V. and Merrill Bonarrigo founded Messina Hof Vineyard in 1977 in Bryan, Texas, as pioneers of the Texas grape and wine industries. Today, Messina Hof has four wineries around Texas and continues to be one of the most awarded wineries in Texas in regional, national, and international competitions. The Messina Hof legacy continues with their son, Paul, and his wife, Karen.

Paul V. Bonarrigo, born in the shadow of Yankee Stadium and graduated from Columbia University, served in the Navy during Vietnam, and studied winemaking at the University of California–Davis while stationed in California. Merrill Bonarrigo, a native of Bryan–College Station, Texas, graduated from Texas A&M University with a degree in business management and taught Wine Retailing at University of Houston.

Paul and Merrill introduced Sagrantino grapes to Texas. They have traveled to thirty-eight countries to teach wine hospitality and successful generational transition. They lead wine tour groups around the world, blog, and author books:

> *Ultimate Food and Wine Pairing Cookbook*
>
> *Ultimate Food and Wine Pairing Cookbook II*
>
> *Vineyard Cuisine, Meals, and Memories from Messina Hof*
>
> *Family, Tradition and Romance—The Messina Hof Story*
>
> *Curse of Estacado—The Trail of Blood and Wine*
>
> *Blood on the Brazos – The Trail of Blood and Wine*